D0962061

Henry & Eva

and the FAMOUS PEOPLE GHOSTS

Also by Andrea Portes

Henry & Eva and the Castle on the Cliff

Henry & Eva

and the FAMOUS PEOPLE GHOSTS

Andrea Portes

HARPER
An Imprint of HarperCollinsPublishers

Henry & Eva and the Famous People Ghosts
Copyright © 2019 by Andrea Portes
Interior illustrations by Sonia Kretschmar
Border by Kanunnikov Pavlo / Shutterstock
All rights reserved. Printed in the United States of America. No part of
this book may be used or reproduced in any manner whatsoever without
written permission except in the case of brief quotations embodied in
critical articles and reviews. For information address HarperCollins
Children's Books, a division of HarperCollins Publishers, 195 Broadway,
New York, NY 10007.
www.harpercollinschildrens.com
ISBN 978-0-06-256004-9
Typography by Michelle Taormina
19 20 21 22 23   PC/LSCH   10 9 8 7 6 5 4 3 2 1

First Edition

For my adorable son, Wyatt, and all his ragamuffin friends

May you build Lego kingdoms, skip stones, play hide-and-seek, roller-skate at Moonlight Rollerway, play little league at Silverlake Rec, catch hermit crabs in Cape Cod, build frog cities in Door County, design lizard hotels in the San Gabriel creeks, giggle at Bob Baker Marionette Theater, rattle off the heroes of Olympus, build rocket ships out of cardboard boxes, and wield your Harry Potter wands for eternity. If I could capture you all in a snow globe, I would hand you to the gods and say, "You see, this is why we must save the world."

Henry & Eva

and the FAMOUS PEOPLE GHOSTS

PART ONE

1

I'VE ALWAYS ENJOYED listening to people fight. Not physical fighting, of course. What do you take me for, some kind of brute? No, no. I am talking about the kind of fighting you hear if, say, you are on a road trip with your family and suddenly, somewhere between Carlsbad and Yellowstone, you decide to pull over for the night at random motel number 536, always with a flickering neon sign, a slightly bored lady at the front desk, and a painting above the beds of either a seascape, usually with seagulls, or a landscape, usually with mountains and possibly a deer.

None of this art is going to make it into the MoMA, incidentally, but I do find it oddly comforting.

I'm speaking about word-fights. Especially the fights

between couples. Fascinating. There I would sit, ear to the wall, trying to discern every tone, every accusation, every rebuttal, piecing it together like puzzles on *Blue's Clues*. What does it mean? Why is she so mad? It seems like he's really trying. Is this the end? Will they make up? Or have they had enough?

You would think, after my twelve years of motel fight investigations, that I would be able to remember a single fight that ended with agreement and cheerful banter. But never. I'm not sure if that's because arguments in motel rooms are doomed from the start, or maybe if, perhaps, I just wasn't close enough to actually hear the reconciliation. Because it was a hug. Or a tender look. Or a hand gesture. Something I couldn't hear through the paper-thin wall.

Henry, of course, has always considered this habit of mine to be crass and beneath me. And he's probably right. But just because a person is right does not mean they are going to dampen my morbid curiosity.

And as it so happens, my morbid curiosity, in this case, turns out to be more of a plus than a negative. Not a saving grace. Not a miracle, mind you. But just helpful. A helpful bad habit.

I bet you are wondering what I am even talking about. That's okay. I wonder that a lot of times, too. The worst time to wonder that, I have learned on my twelve years on Earth, is in the middle of a sentence. Because you know you have to complete the sentence, but you are working with nothing. There is just nothing in there to grab. Yet you must power through. You must solve the mystery of what is coming out of your mouth by the end of the sentence. A daunting challenge.

Of course, this never happens to Henry. His sentences, if they come out at all, come out in logical phrases or even paragraphs, perfectly pieced together, subject verb predicate, with the fastidiousness of Daniel Webster or Hermione Granger. Which is why it's not always the easiest for Henry to make friends. I mean, does anybody ever really want to compete, voluntarily, with that?

As it turns out, yes.

You see, something strange happened last year, near the middle of the year. Something mysterious indeed.

Henry, my brother, made a friend.

And this friend was not what you thought he'd be. You see, if I had constructed from my imagination the perfect friend for Henry, I would have probably imagined a glasses-wearing, redheaded, freckled, slightly pudgy, possibly nose-picking boy named Harold, or Igby.

But that is not who turned up at all.

One day, in early September, Henry showed up at the house with what looked, and still looks, like one-fifth of a boy band. A person who was sporting a blond mop of hair, almost a surfer cut, with, get this, *blue streaks*. Checkered Vans, skinny distressed jeans, a jean jacket with a faded cityscape on the back—and a love of magic, Legos, Rube Goldberg contraptions, and a continuous smile on his face. A happy-go-lucky kid. A funny kid. A smart kid. A witty kid.

A kid with a very strange name.

Henry did not tell us, any of us, not Marisol, not Claude, not Terri, that he would be coming home with this new BFF. Or that he even had this new BFF. The whole thing was thrust upon us, and we were to make sense of it what we would.

I just walked in the kitchen and there they were, *avec* ant farm, peering into the tiny corridors and passageways constructed by the ants.

Marisol and I stood there, speechless, trying to understand what this meant, what this could mean, what this should mean. But to no avail. Their interest in the ants was tantamount.

You're probably wondering why I am telling you this. Welp, ladies and germs, there's a *reason* for the new friend. None of the things later could have happened, or would have happened, without both Henry making said friend and us finding said friend in our kitchen, wondering if he'd gotten lost on his way to some super-cool activity like DJ Skillz class or Future Leaders of Greenpeace.

Just as a Ferris wheel ascends and descends on each little cog and screw . . . this little tale lies firmly on the axis of Henry's new friend and my essentially limited spying ability.

I should catch you up, though. We should all be looking at the same slate. You see, it's not a blank one. No, no.

Hmm . . . how to tell the story of two kids, five ghosts, and one villain? Concisely, I suppose. In a manner of expedience.

You see, last summer, something very strange happened, and it did not happen to mermaids in the middle of Muskogee or chupacabras from the oil fields of Texas or unicorns from the lost city of Atlantis. Nope. It happened to us. And I couch it like that because, let's face it, it seems unlikely. Like a fairy tale. Or a myth. Or a spooky campfire story. And in some ways I wish it was. Because part of it is sad and horrible.

But not every part.

Part of it is also wondrous and amazing. Sublime. Like life. Part awful, part beautiful. Almost like you can't have one without the other. A payment. A tally. A scale. The Ferris ride, itself, pointless if it doesn't go down before going up, or vice versa. I mean, honestly, who would ride a Ferris wheel if you just had to sit there? You wouldn't even pay for the ticket!

"Here, can I pay you three tickets just so I can sit here like a rump roast?"

No. There has to be both the up part and the down part. So, here we go . . . we'll start with the down.

Last year, before the end of the school year, our parents died. And they didn't just die, they were in a "boating accident." Yet it wasn't just a boating accident. But a setup. You see, we had an uncle who decided that money mattered more than love, or decency, or morality, for that matter, and his greed drove him to get rid of our parents in the hope that he would inherit our rather old Victorian house perched oh-so-precariously on the side of a cliff in Big Sur.

Now, this house has been in the family since the gold rush. Yes, 1849. But our uncle decided *he* should inherit it and, more important, the land underneath it, so he could sell it and run off with the money, which he probably would have blown, let's face it, in two years. Now, I'm not going to tell you which uncle it was. Because that would be giving away the ghost.

However, I will tell you this, this fact, which you probably won't believe until you witness it. That's fine. I'm not mad. I wouldn't believe it, either. I mean, I would be crossing my arms at this, immediately.

But the simple fact of the matter is that by the end of this great tragedy, or mystery, or whatever you wish to call it, my brother and I inherited a kind of superpower. I know, I know. You still don't believe me. But it's true. No matter how far-fetched or "Northern California" it may sound. Okay, ready? The superpower is . . .

My brother and I can see ghosts.

And not just see them, we can communicate with them. Like talk to them. In detail. Long conversations. Witty banter. Jokes. What have you. It's actually a pretty fascinating skill because, unlike in movies or books, you get to go back in time through someone's actual memory and learn what it was like, say, when the Donner party was found, or when the *Titanic* sank, or when the Wright brothers flew a plane up from the beaches of Kitty Hawk.

It's not superstrength, or invisibility, or the power of flight, but it's not bad.

Still, I understand. You don't believe me. And that's fine.

You'll see.

In the meantime I should probably tell you where we are. And what we are doing here. And why this night will forever take the cake as the weirdest, most dangerous, most perilous night of all time.

And yes, there will be ghosts.

2

REMEMBER WHEN I was telling you about Henry's new friend? I mean, you must. It wasn't that long ago, jeez.

Well, I'm going to tell you a few facts now about said friend. And I urge you to hold your judgment until the end of the fact parade.

Fact number one: He's from LA.

I know, I know. But don't hate him. I know everybody from LA is supposed to be stupid and vapid and think that Chekhov is only a character from *Star Trek*. It is supposed to be the land of plastic surgery, palm trees, swimming pools, and movie stars. But I will tell you one or two things I have learned from our new friend—sushi burritos. And Korean tacos. And tofu, just straight from the box. Even seaweed. The crinkly kind. Also,

I have never seen someone who cared less about what people look like. No, really.

Have you ever noticed how sometimes adults seem surprised at what people look like in relation to what they are? Like, say, where they are from? You know, on the globe? Or in their background. Like, if they meet Marisol, who hails originally from Guatemala, they sometimes start speaking English in an overemphasized manner? As if she won't understand? Or if, say, they meet someone who is Asian and they ask them where they're from and seem surprised if they say, like, San Jose? So, that quality, even on the smallest, most minuscule level . . . seems to be completely absent from Henry's new friend. It's almost as if he could meet someone purple, from the planet Zorth, and not skip a beat. He'd just say, "Wanna build a fort?" and that would be that.

Is this, I wonder, a product of his LA upbringing? A natural consequence of growing up in a place where the corner-mall signs are in Armenian, Spanish, Chinese, Yiddish, Russian, Taiwanese, Tagalog, Japanese, Vietnamese, French, and maybe English?

Is "different" just "normal" for him? Like, for most people, having a library or a post office?

This trait, I've decided, is my favorite trait of the new friend.

And now, for his name:

Zeb.

Yup. A country-sounding name. A western name. A name that makes you think he should be riding horses. And maybe lassoing something. A name meaning he should be wearing a shirt with mother-of-pearl snaps. Maybe cowboy boots. But in reality, he's a total city slicker.

Our aunt Terri seems to think that Zeb is the cutest thing to walk the earth since ladybugs. She even buys him stuff if we are out somewhere there is stuff to be bought. But, let's face it, she really likes buying stuff. So, she'll buy a trinket for me, a trinket for Henry, *and a trinket for Zeb*. As if somehow, this boy, this new boy, is her adopted son. A son from out west. A son she could teach all her lasso tricks to and tell stories to by the fire, in front of a spit. A shooting star flying over them.

Our uncle Claude, on the other hand, seems confused by Zeb and his blue streaks. Why, exactly, *does* he have blue streaks in his hair? Where did they come from? What are they *for*? When I explain to Claude that they are an expression of his individuality, the sides of Claude's lips go down, as if in doubt. I say, "Don't you see, Claude? It's a way of him saying not all is as it should be?" And Claude will say, "Is that it? Sounds pretty profound of a statement for an eleven-year-old." And then I, too, will doubt my assessment. Maybe sometimes a blue streak is only a blue streak. Nothing more. The kind of thing you would just randomly have if you were from LA.

I'll tell you this. None of the kids our age, here in Big Sur, have them. It wouldn't even occur to them.

Now the third fact: He met Henry because both he and Henry were separated in their school for being weird. Now, when I say weird, maybe you will think that's a bad thing, or a derogative thing, but really it just means that they have a tendency to tinker, experiment, and investigate when they are supposed to be listening. The problem, according to the teachers, seems to be that they aren't paying the necessary attention to the matter at hand. However, I think the problem is that the matter at hand doesn't have enough to do with the solar robot they are building out of a tin can they found in the garbage.

I, for one, am just happy Henry has a playmate who is just as interested in ant farms, potion-making, and flying-robot-building as he is. Because now these things don't need to be handled alone.

Simply speaking, two weirds make a right.

You may be wondering why this aforementioned Zeb happens to be in Big Sur in the first place. Quite frankly, Big Sur is more of a travel destination than a place to move to. A place people come to from all corners of the country to freak out on the steep, winding roads snuggled between the cliffs and the perilous sea hundreds of feet below. A place to go whale watching. A place to eat dinner at that wooden restaurant on the cliff nestled in the middle of all the eucalyptus trees. A tourist place.

But it just so happens that Zeb's dad is a journalist, tried and true, and was asked to become the editor in chief of the *Monterey Herald*. Now, as far as fast-breaking news organizations go, this doesn't feel like much. But there is a second topping to this here ice-cream cone, which is that Zeb's parents are divorced. So he splits his time between Big Sur with his dad and Carmel-by-the-Sea with his mom, who I know nothing about so stop asking.

And, from what I gather, Zeb has no interest in talking about it, either. It seems to roll off him like everything else, an afterthought. Like, yeah, that happened, but let's get back to this Lego contraption I just created with flashing lights that is capable of nuclear fusion. That is what we are doing here! He doesn't want people to feel sorry for him or say "di-vorce" in a weird whisper and make a sad face at him. He just wants to treat it like the sun coming up in the east, and the moss growing on the north side of the trees. A simple fact. Nothing more. Nothing to interrupt his experiments.

So the Monterey paper job isn't exactly a stepping-stone to Reuters. But Zeb's journalist dad seems content to manage the paper, in this beautiful place, this quiet but tranquil nest. He can do that here. Just be at peace.

Except that *now* he's getting married. Which I think is a sort of wrench in the works. I'm fairly sure that was not part of his quiet, bucolic plan. In fact, I'm fairly sure it was a surprise to everyone involved, including Zeb.

Now, the entire reason for this long and possibly drawn-out explanation is that tonight, the night in question, takes place on the wedding night of said dad and new bride. A night where seemingly all the men and women from Cayucos to Bodega Bay have gathered to celebrate the nuptials of Zeb's dad and a woman named Binky. I have not yet determined if this is her real name or the shortening of a longer name, such as Belinda or Elizabeth or Beatrice. But she was introduced as Binky and she's on the ivory engraved wedding invitation as Binky, so I would say she's all in as far as that is concerned.

The location, on said ivory wedding invitation, was enough to make us gasp, as it is the first time anyone I have ever met or heard of has ever attempted, or even thought to attempt, such a feat. You see, it's a grand affair. A bit grander than I would have imagined Zeb's quiet, dignified, discerning dad to find acceptable.

And Zeb, of course, just shrugs about it. You know Zeb.

I can only imagine this is Binky's doing. An idea she had that was worthy of someone named Binky. A grand idea. A showstopping idea. An idea as if to say, "I have arrived. I am here! Observe me! Respect me! Quake in my presence! For I am Binky!"

Because, you see, the place for these nuptials is not a quaint little white-clad church, or a rustic seaside affair with a clam-bake and maybe tiki torches for the reception.

Nope.

The location of the wedding is none other than:

Hearst Castle.

It's okay, I'll wait. You can look it up.

3

SO, YOU'VE SEEN it now? Hearst Castle? Great. So, let's unpack this for a minute, shall we? Hearst Castle is a giant, absurd, bajillion-dollar place, perched atop a vast stretch of land on the California Central Coast. Now, most people think of traffic or movies when they think of California, but this is the rolling hills, unspoiled, wine-country part of California that kind of looks like the south of France. It is all protected, so no giant hotels everywhere. Many people, in fact, from other countries who come to the States, if they find themselves on this particular stretch of road, between Morro Bay and Monterey . . . pretty much freak out. Like they never thought this country of ours had such a hidden jewel. And this is something everyone in California is desperately trying to keep this way.

But I digress. So, this is what happened. In 1865, George Hearst purchased 40,000 acres of land on the aforementioned rolling hills. After his mother's death in 1919, William Randolph Hearst inherited said thousands of acres of this land, and over time, he purchased more. Eventually he owned about 250,000 acres. With architect Julia Morgan, Hearst dreamed up a little haven he called La Cuesta Encantada—which translates to "Enchanted Hill." By 1947, Hearst's health faltered and he had to leave the remote location, because it really was in the middle of nowhere and if he got sick, he'd be pretty much out of luck.

So even though the estate comprised 165 rooms and 123 acres of gardens, terraces, pools, and walkways—all built to Hearst's specifications and showcasing a legendary art collection consisting of everything from Egyptian antiquities, to Roman and Greek sculptures, to whatever was the most expensive anything old William Randolph could buy—to this day it is still unfinished. Sidebar: Apparently he detested modern art. So, if you're looking for anything abstract, you've come to the wrong castle.

So this lonely, classical art–stuffed, Spanish Revival castle sits looking across the Pacific Ocean like a great Sphinx confused by the riddle of its existence. And, you, too, can see it for the ticket price of $25 or $12 depending on how old you are. Because now it's a museum. I am unaffiliated with and not compensated by said estate, but I'd say it's worth the trip.

Although, to be honest, our tour of the place seems a bit whitewashed. Hearst, in the audio guide, comes off as kind of a hero. While Henry called the place "an unexamined slobbering rant of conspicuous consumption." And I can't help agreeing. Keep in mind, this guy, Hearst, built this huge temple to avarice smack-dab in the middle of the Great Depression. While there were soup-kitchen lines around the block, tent cities called Hoovervilles, and mothers unable to feed their starving children.

So, I am just going to give that ranting Hearst tour a rating of "Ahem." One star.

However, I forgot the best part. Over the years, in its heyday, it was considered very awesome to be invited to said conspicuous castle by old Billy, and here is a list of some folks who were lucky enough to win that golden ticket:

Winston Churchill

Howard Hughes

Charles Lindbergh

George Bernard Shaw

Charlie Chaplin

Gary Cooper

Joan Crawford

Douglas Fairbanks Jr.

Errol Flynn

Clark Gable

Greta Garbo

Cary Grant

Buster Keaton

Harpo Marx

Groucho Marx

Now, most of these were stars of silent film back in the day, so you probably have never heard of them. But believe me, at the time, this would've been like having a couple of friends over for the weekend and it would be like, "Pass the peas, Beyoncé." Oh, and, "I'm not sure you've met my friend Leonardo DiCaprio but he has the best story about the time we almost tripped off Randolph's boat!"

Like that.

So you see, the idea of having your wedding at said absurd castle is, well, *absurd*. I mean, *seriously*.

But Binky seems to be the straw that stirs the drink.

I bet you're wondering what Binky looks like. Well, it's not what you think. She has long chestnut hair that she often wears in braids. Her feet are frequently shod in clogs. Also, she wears glasses. So, again, the Hearst Castle thing is totally unexpected. She could, I suppose, take off those glasses, clogs, and braids and be a hotty-potatty but I haven't seen any indication of hotty-potattyness so far, glasses or no.

So why Hearst?

Here is a discussion I had with Henry about said mystery:

"Okay, so, Henry. Don't you find this a bit strange?"

"Find what?"

"This whole Hearst Castle wedding thing . . . I mean, don't you find it a bit out of character?"

"Perhaps." Henry thinks. "However, it does happen to be filled with antiquities from both the Assyrian and Sumerian civilizations, and she does have her PhD in classics from Bryn Mawr, arguably the best graduate program in the country on the matter. My deduction is it's simply a love of Mesopotamian fertility figures and artifacts from the Silk Road that prompted the choice."

"But it seems so . . . gaudy," I add.

"I suppose, if you think an interest in the ancient empires, from the Anunnaki to the fall of Rome is . . . gaudy. I find it fascinating! What there is to be learned from the fall of empires!"

"That's just what I mean. This *is* the fall of Rome. So decadent!"

Henry shrugs. "It's Binky's wedding. Not yours."

Touché.

Henry goes back to his magnet experiment. He is trying to create a portal using magnets and the frequencies found in the lines of a mandala. I know. I give him about ten months until we're stepping into the multiverse. We can study their empires then.

While Henry's point is true, this still doesn't quite square with the finances of an ancient antiquities scholar (Binky) and a small-town newspaper chief (Zeb's dad). Sure, Binky has written a few books on the matter. *Assyrians and the Invention of Cruelty, Egypt: Racism Beyond the Nile,* and her most famous, *Aristotle and the Seeds of Slavery.* But all those books are just boring enough to be *important.* And *important* doesn't necessarily translate to massive wealth.

I can only assume Binky comes from a rich family. And she would have to. I mean, her name *is* Binky. Not exactly a moniker from the mean streets of Hardscrabble, USA. In Hardscrabble, you'd probably get beat up a lot for a name like that. By your own relatives.

All of this is really just a preamble to the feeling I have at this very moment, which can best be described as, "Why am I here?"

Because you see, where we are, Henry and I, is about fifteen rows back from Zeb, who is basically starring in this wedding, as the eleven-year-old best man to his father. And above us are soaring rafters with gold gilded everything, red velvet everything else, and Greco-Roman statues everywhere. Popping out of the woodwork. Practically falling out of the windows. It's as if at any moment one of them is just going to grab my hand and say, "Get me out of here!"

I vow to help, if necessary.

If you're wondering where our beloved uncle Claude and aunt Terri are, the answer is, they dropped us off here with Marisol. They showered us with kisses and hugs, scruffed us on the hair, and then took off to Paris. Yes, just like that. I'm not sure, exactly, why Paris, except that Terri said something about shopping and romance and nonrefundable tickets. In that order.

You may be wondering where Marisol is, and that's where I look like a jerk. You see, Marisol has decided to get her pilot's license. I have to say, I'm confident in her abilities as she has always been an excellent driver. But it takes lots of hours; pilots call it "logging hours." To get said license. So, I sorta kinda told Marisol we've got this covered so she can fly off into the great blue sky and someday become a commercial pilot, which, let's face it, would be awesome. I would give a thousand dollars just to hear her voice come over the airplane intercom. "Hallo, dees is jour captain e-speaking. Our flight time is e-six hours today." Also, I have this feeling Marisol will somehow end up the head of the airline. She's just that person.

My imaginary dreamscape of Marisol at the head of the United Airlines boardroom table is interrupted by the melancholy sounds of the string quartet playing Mozart, because that has to happen. I mean, no string quartet, no wedding. Everyone is sort of looking around, looking at the program, looking at each other, giving a few kind nods, wedding nods, this is a happy occasion. There are a few confused folks near the back who seem to be wondering if they are in the wrong place—not because they are here for a tour, as Binky rented out the entirety of the place, which must have cost a king's ransom, but because it's just such a ludicrous, luxurious place to celebrate anything, really.

It's not a perfect day for a wedding. Not a bright blue day. More of a *hmm-it-might-rain* sort of day. Now, in most places that might just mean maybe grab an umbrella or wear your galoshes. Not around here though. The last time it rained and rained and rained, they had to shut down the Pacific Coast Highway, also known as *the only way in and out of Big Sur*. Supplies needed to be airlifted in till the road was fixed. So, a little rain is fun, but a lot of rain is, well, not so fun.

That might be part of the nervous energy. Or maybe it's because Zeb's dad just met Binky about six months ago, so that's not exactly a lengthy courtship.

Zeb's mom is already remarried to a "venture capitalist." I'm not sure what it means, but one time Zeb referred to him as a "vulture capitalist" so that doesn't sound good. Henry said when Zeb went to visit his mom and his "new dad," there was not a detail left unchecked in the fun department. Pool? Check. Tree house? Check. Air hockey table? Check. Batting cage? Check. Foosball table? Check. Pool table? Check. Giant play-room full of Zeb's experiments and Lego creations? Check. Elaborate train set around the whole yard? Check and check.

So, whatever it is that this "vulture capitalist" does . . . it seems to be working out.

There is something else that's a little off, too. When we were coming up the tram to this here Hearst Castle, there were loads and loads of trucks. Flower trucks. Catering trucks. Entertain-ment trucks. Linen trucks. I mean . . . so many trucks. It was like a truck convention. I had the distinct thought that there must be about a million people coming to the wedding, or at least a thousand.

And yet.

When we reached the chapel itself, which is more of a cathedral than a chapel, really, there were only about one hundred guests. Yes, one hundred guests, of which Henry and I make two. So ninety-eight guests besides us, but let's not get bogged down with the minutiae here. The point is . . . that sure seems like a lot of trucks for one hundred guests. Not that I'm a wedding planner or anything.

I mentioned it to Henry and this was about how that went:

Me: "Doesn't that seem like a lot of trucks for this many people?"

Henry: "Hmm. Interesting observation. I can only assume that Binky has decided to attend to every detail in the most elaborate way possible."

Me: "But why? It's not like Zeb's dad cares. I mean, he's so crunchy his Birkenstocks practically navigate themselves to the nearest protest."

Henry: "Amusing. Perhaps her great family wealth has put him on par with his ex-wife's new husband, the venture capitalist, who is clearly part of the one percent. It's possible this is a kind of sweet revenge."

Me: "Well, what does Zeb have to say about it?"

Henry: "Not much. Although I do think he enjoys his new waterslide. And I don't blame him. There is a kind of reckless glee in flinging oneself onto it."

And at this moment, the embodiment of reckless flinging pokes his head between us.

"Mini sushirritos, anyone?"

It's Zeb, offering a small plate of tiny sushi burritos to us, his face a big pumpkin smile.

"I'd offer the mini Korean tacos, but they're harder to eat. Like, I've had to change my shirt twice."

"Ooo, thanks, Zeb. That's nice of you."

"I just don't want you guys to die of boredom. This may take a while. Also, I'm supposed to do a reading and it's so cheesy I know I'm going to laugh."

"What? You can't laugh!" I say, amused.

"Well, what exactly is it?" Henry asks.

"Put it this way, at some point I am supposed to say 'Love is like a salad.'"

Henry and I both stifle a laugh.

"You should just say love is like a sushi burrito," Henry whispers.

"No! A Korean taco. It's messy!" I add.

The three of us try to keep it down, though our pew neighbors are clearly starting to get annoyed.

Zeb's dad waves him back from the altar and Zeb gives us a shrug, heading back. As he goes, he gestures around at the vast, excessive cathedral and rolls his eyes, as if to say, "Isn't this all ridiculous?"

We nod back, smiling in accordance. It's so hard to not like him. You could drop him anywhere and he'd just kind of go with it, like, "Oh, yeah. Okay, this is what we're doing. Cool."

But for some reason it angers me. Zeb's ability to navigate the world with such carefree abandon. Maybe I'm jealous. Maybe I'm too stressed out. Maybe I'm too lame. That is a definite possibility. It's a mystery. Like the great pyramids of Giza. Or the stones at Puma Punku. Or why Trader Joe's parking lots are always so squirrelly.

The music has been going on for a while, but according to the program the wedding party doesn't start their march in until "Pachelbel's Canon." So, we are all in an essential holding pattern.

Maybe I can dazzle my brother with some knowledge about this place that I gained from an intense study of the Googles. "Henry, did you know they have a bunch of statues here from Egypt?"

"Yes. Four pieces, exactly, of art dated from the New Kingdom. In the middle is Sekhmet, which translates to 'the powerful,' depicted with the body of a woman and the head of a lioness. She was portrayed as the bloodthirsty protector of Ra, the sun god."

Of course. Because *Henry*.

"If you're curious about the New Kingdom, sometimes referred to as the Egyptian Empire, it was the period in ancient Egyptian history between the sixteenth century BC and the eleventh century BC, covering the Eighteenth, Nineteenth, and Twentieth Dynasties of Egypt."

"Uh, sure."

Henry smiles.

"Well, I for one am looking forward to seeing these statues. Who could resist the bloodthirsty protector of the sun god?"

A hush falls over the crowd, and then it starts—"Pachelbel's Canon."

"A bit somber for a wedding, really," Henry says. "I suppose Binky finds the traditional 'Wedding March' passé."

Henry's probably right. He seems to really have an instinct when it comes to Binky. A sort of attention out of character for him. Wait a minute. Does my brother, Henry, have a little crush on Binky?

The officiant, who I'm told is a Unitarian Universalist, steps humbly up to the altar.

Zeb's dad steps out to the altar from the side, wearing a black-and-white tuxedo, looking a bit sheepish.

And now Zeb steps out as well. The best man. Maybe it is a bit unusual to have your son as the best man, but what else was he going to be? The ring bearer? Too old. An usher? Too vague. Almost an insult for your own son, really. I get the feeling his dad is trying to make this as easy as possible for Zeb. A transition that won't traumatize him. But with Zeb trauma doesn't seem to be a factor.

The melancholy canon continues and so does the parade down the aisle of whoever all these people are. I peer through the many heads bobbing up and around, in assorted curiosity and awe, to catch Zeb there, at the altar, next to his dad. He gives a funny little nod. An acknowledgment of the pomp of this matrimony. And I feel a funny thing then, almost a sense of relief. Yes, this is all very expensive. And yes, this is all very glamorous and gold-gilded and all the rest of the words involving a *G* and an *L*. But somehow, Zeb's attitude, the way he takes it . . . is a license not to care. And with that license not to care is a kind of freedom.

The procession comes to an end and then we are left in the moment of sort of forced anticipation. I can't help but think there is a kind of hold here. A moment to prepare us for the almost certain collective gasp we obviously will be having at first glance of the bride. Of Binky!

Henry whispers into my ear, "Is there a purpose to this somewhat elongated pause?"

"I think the purpose is for us to freak out," I whisper back.

Henry smiles. I've always enjoyed making my kid brother laugh, or smile, or demonstrate any kind of amusement. You see, he is a fragile, focused, sometimes brooding little boy, and it's important for me to make life less serious. Our parents' death didn't help. And my job as the mood lightener became all the more important then. Keeping us happy, shining. I know our mom would've wanted it that way. When we were growing up, if we felt like we'd disappointed them, my mom would always say, "Oh, honey. Your father and I just want you to be healthy and happy and kind. That's all we care about. That's the most important thing, in the end." If she were talking to Henry she would say, "No squinty eyes. You're much too handsome to brood. I won't allow it!" And, of course, then Henry would smile and blush.

Ah, speaking of blushing, here she is! The beautiful blushing bride! Well, look at her. There's no denying she really put something into this. And, I have to admit, I've never seen anything like this dress before. It has embroidered lace around the neck, and all around the body, but then there's a kind of downward triangle from the collarbone to the waist, pointing to the floor, sleeves that kind of look like butterflies, then the same lace going down tight, but somehow there is flowing involved. Maybe the butterflies are the flowy part? I get it. Her brunette hair is cascading down around everything and she could practically be on the cover of *Paris Bride* magazine, if that even exists. If it doesn't, it exists in my imagination and is therefore existent in some form. Either way, she has earned the collective gasp she was setting us all up to inhale. It is a synchronistic breath of exultation and awe. Binky has done it!

I notice, slightly annoyed, that even Henry has fallen into this heaped enchantment. Henry! And, peeking out at the altar, I see both Zeb and his dad, mesmerized, too. Zeb's dad even seems to have a tear in his eye. Zeb is looking, too, but it's more of a sense of interest. A taking in. I wonder if one day he'll be a painter. That seems like a fit. Irreverent but somehow in love with the world and all the myriad of treasures in it.

As Binky makes it to the altar the officiant clears his throat rather unceremoniously and begins orating his notes. I pretend to contemplate the names and songs in the program but am roused out of my ruse by a hush falling over the crowd, a shared silence and shock I haven't heard since, well, forever really.

Even Henry stands like a stone.

I look up to see the last thing you would ever expect to see at an occasion as sumptuous as this.

There, do you see it? There, at the back of the chapel. An old man, an elderly man, covered in dirt and mud, clothes in tatters.

One by one each head turns to take in the man, until even the officiant, the bride, and the groom look back to see what on Earth has charged the ions in the room to this massive extent. As if an invisible dark cloud has just overtaken us.

The man comes forward, bent over, in silence. For some reason, everyone just keeps staring, allowing this stillness. Maybe to say something is to admit that it's happening, and nobody wants to be the first one to acknowledge it, because it seems like a mirage.

Finally, the disheveled man reaches the front of the aisle, the altar, and he looks up to the officiant. A different kind of gasp now than the one reserved for the beauty of the bride. This, a horrified one. The man, his face bruised and bloodied. His left eye swollen, almost to the extent of not seeming like an eye at all.

Zeb's dad protectively steps forward, stands in front of his bride and his son.

The man looks up, stunned, as if he had no idea where he was in the first place.

"Please, please, sir . . ."

The officiant breaks through. "What is it, my son? What has happened?"

"It's . . . it's . . ."

And then the man promptly falls to the ground.

4

I'M FAIRLY SURE this wasn't part of the wedding plan.

Yes, we'll have lilies, roses, posies, and hydrangea, all in different hues of white and ivory. Yes, we'll have the guests' greeting after the ceremony with champagne. Yes, we'll have a string quartet begin fifteen minutes before the procession. And, also, if you don't mind, I'd like a sullied, beaten stranger to collapse at the altar just as the nuptials begin!

But Binky is not pouting, she is looking concerned, just as her soon-to-be husband is, leaning over the wounded man with a glass of water. Zeb hands over a shawl, a kind gesture from one of the guests. The shawl is immediately put over the injured man, making him look like a crippled bird in a sequined gown.

After being sat up and tended to, the man revives. Looking up, meekly.

"I'm so sorry. I didn't know . . . I didn't know what to do . . ."

"Please, what is the matter?" The officiant leans in.

"They've taken over."

The officiant and Zeb's dad share a look. What exactly does that mean?

Zeb stands, looking curious, next to Binky, who is the picture of concern. I have to hand it to her, most brides would not be enjoying this particular melodrama in the middle of their gorgeous wedding.

"I'm sorry, who? Who has taken over? Where?" The officiant leans in farther, puzzled.

"Ragged Point."

There's a stunned silence.

Now, for those of you who do not hail from this blustery part of the coast, Ragged Point is the beginning of the road to Big Sur. It's a tiny hamlet of a town, consisting of only one inn, one restaurant, a gift shop, a gas station, and even a wedding chapel. Why does it exist? Welp, the million-dollar views seem to be the reason. It's a romantic spot perched just before the treacherous winding road above the cliffs and is considered the gateway to Big Sur. It's twenty minutes north of San Simeon on the PCH, making it the perfect hotel for tourists visiting Hearst Castle.

Now, the idea of taking over a town seems absurd, but not

absurd enough that the guests, many of whom are actually staying in the one inn at Ragged Point, would not see this as seriously unfunny. It has been isolated before. During the mudslides. During the fires. After an earthquake. It's not the best place to get a signal, whether you have Sprint, Verizon, AT&T, T-Mobile, or anything less than a satellite dish for a head. And it's the kind of place where people generally leave their doors open.

But a town being *taken over*? In this day and age? I mean, this sounds more like a 1910 thing. Or even 1810. *Them banditos have come and taken over the dadgum town!* I mean, right?

And, also, what would you want with a *town*? I mean, there is infrastructure to maintain, community services to provide, water filtration maintenance. Sounds like a big pain.

Zeb's dad keeps his voice calm. "Excuse me? I'm not sure I heard you correctly. Did you say—"

"Yes, yes, they've taken over the town! All of it. Everyone there locked up! The men, the women . . . even the children! Locked up behind the Blue Heron, they've got them in that shed like animals! It's horrible. Just horrible. I tried to save them but . . . well, look at me. I'm an old man. 'Old goat,' they called me."

"Who?! Who did this?"

"These men, a group of them . . . who knows where they came from? Now they're just looting the place!"

A shudder goes through the crowd as everyone considers the fate of the women and children locked up behind the Blue Heron.

No, no, it can't be. Something must be done.

"And these men? What did they look like?"

"Oh, they were different. They were . . . I don't even know if they were speaking English."

"What language were they speaking?" The officiant leans in again.

Something about this irks Zeb's dad. "Excuse me, I'm not sure I see the point in—"

"I'm just trying to figure out what we're up against!"

And that is the first it dawns on anybody that *we* are up against anyone.

Henry turns to me. "'We'? What does he mean, 'we'?"

The men from the crowd seem to be moving forward, a tide of agitation. I can't tell whether they're worried about their hotel rooms and what might be in them, or about the people left in the town. Maybe a combination of both . . . ?

Suddenly the tide swells.

"We must do something!"

"We have to go down there!"

"What about the police?!"

That freezes the momentum. Oh, yeah, the police. Right. We don't live in a postapocalyptic dystopian afterscape where every man must fend for himself. Not yet anyway. So, of course, there are police. And, if movies teach us anything, it's that this is a job for the police.

"Right! The police! Call the police! Where are they?"

The man looks up. "We tried, all the phones are down. The

wires cut. The one cell tower destroyed. That's why I came here. Thank God you're all here." Now he looks up at the concerned bride. Binky, nodding in empathy. "I thought it would be closed today, this place. This is a blessing. Your wedding is a blessing."

Zeb's dad reaches a hand out to squeeze Binky's hand. I think the squeeze means, "I'm sorry our lavish wedding is ruined, honey. But this is an emergency and thank you for taking it so well." She puts her hand on his. Yes, it's okay. The wedding is, indeed, ruined. But, also indeed, we have to help.

"Um, has anyone ever heard of a cell phone?" It's a girl in the front row, someone's annoyed daughter, obviously upset at having to be here in the first place. She takes out her cell and becomes increasingly less confident as she realizes it's not working.

"Um, does *anybody* have a signal?" she asks, more polite now.

Everyone digs into their purses, blazers, and pockets, finding their phones. Trying them. Realizing it's no use.

Zeb's dad takes the floor. "Okay, so obviously there's something wrong with the cell phone service. Maybe the weather."

"Not the weather! Like I said, they destroyed the towers! Cut the lines!" The stranger yelps. Excited again. The officiant tries to calm him.

"What now? Does anyone have any suggestions?" Zeb's dad looks around the room.

"What about the police in San Simeon?" a woman in the front row offers.

"Why, they're here. Up here, don't you see?" The stranger looks at her. Why does no one understand?!

And, of course, that's true. As we look around it becomes obvious that this many people, at a gathering up at Hearst Castle, would amount to that kind of security. I mean, it's not every wedding that takes place amid a bajillion dollars' worth of art.

"So, they're here. Of course they are." Zeb's dad turns to Binky.

"We have to help them." She nods, resolved. Zeb continues. "Okay, everyone, let's gather around. Can someone go find the police and security stationed around and tell them what's going on?"

"I'll go!" Zeb steps in.

"Yes, yes. I'll go as well!" Henry steps forward, through the crowd.

"Wait, what?" I grab Henry's arm.

"The least we can do is help round up the police. Who knows where they all are in this behemoth labyrinth."

Now all sorts of people begin coming forward, volunteering themselves for service. Mostly men who seem somehow excited by all of this. Like they're all turning to their wives and girlfriends to say good-bye, and going off to war. Most of the women are standing up, wanting to go with them, but somehow many of them are coaxed into staying.

"No, no, it's not safe."

"No. You have to stay here. It's just, we don't know what we're dealing with."

"Please, you have to stay. This is not the time to have an argument about gender politics!"

I suppose I can see his point, although there is something strange transforming all the men in the room. Seeping into their blood. As if this is the moment they've been waiting for, dying for. A moment to be a hero. Yes, this is the chance!

A kind of befuddlement and resignation on the face of some of the women and children, being sat down and comforted. Somehow, in an emergency, everything has already been settled. Yet there is a resistance among them. A handful of women who are saddling up for this posse, too. One of them already ditched her heels and put on galoshes. (Did she bring galoshes in case of inclement weather? Genius!)

And even I, staring at Henry and Zeb hurrying out of the room, am wondering if I'm meant to stay here. Is that my role? Isn't that what everyone else is doing? Or am I like that woman in galoshes? Hmm.

How to be a girl?

I look around at the stymied faces of the women and children around me. Safe. They are safe. It is settled. I look at Zeb's dad, reasoning with Binky, who is resting on the front pew, stunned. No, no, Binky. This is not how the day was supposed to go.

Then, as if to settle it, drip . . . drip . . . drip. Drip drip. Drip. The final insult. Rain.

Binky exhales, resigned. Okay, now I am starting to feel sorry for her. And she is taking this all really well, considering.

I've seen brides that would have hurled that old man into a planter.

The men and older boys seem to be elbowing their way out in droves. An exodus of exuberant heroism. An army of Dudley Do-Rights heading out to save the day! The resistance women are a little more serious, gearing up for whatever awaits them.

I catch Zeb and Henry hurrying out the back red velvet curtains next to the altar.

And I realize I *am* meant to stay here.

That is what I am *supposed to do.*

But, you see.

I've never, ever been any good at doing what I'm supposed to.

5

THE RAIN IS coming down now, lightly, as if flirting with the idea of really opening up. The sun is starting to set but you can't see it through the clouds; on a clear day you can see every last inch of it sink regally into the ocean, staring out miles and miles over the Pacific, cutting little half-moons in the ocean. But this day doesn't get that kind of blessing. This is a day for madness.

And madness it is, staring out below at the myriad of landings and driveways, the lights and motors of the panoply of cars and trucks on their way down the rolling hill, down from the castle on its perch to the hoi polloi roads below, where the roads lead to streets and the streets lead to highways all the way to the rat races to the north and to the south, San Francisco or Los Angeles, choose your poison.

But the chaos below could rival either metropolis in its current state, everyone running around like chickens with their heads cut off. Bedlam.

And as the lights, motors, cars, and trucks roar down the hill to Ragged Point, I find myself looking around from my perch, finally seeing what is around me. I seem to be in a kind of tangential Roman colonnade. Down below me I can see Henry and Zeb running, yelling to all the men they see who look even vaguely like they are security detail. I mean, I think that last guy was a janitor, really.

They disappear on the other side of the decadent Roman columned pool, out to find more guards, although it does seem like pretty much everyone has been rounded up.

As the sound of the engines wanes down the hill, a kind of quiet takes over. As if all that was just a mad hallucination and we are back to normal once again. The mist is falling over this mini mountain, but it doesn't seem to mind, both the rain and the night enveloping it.

As usual, the cold comes faster than you think when the sun dips down. I've lived here my whole life and it surprises me every time. Mark Twain said the coldest winter he ever spent was a summer in San Francisco. Nobody ever believes it until they get here. How this cold will chill you to the bone, this wet cold off the ocean, up the cliffs.

I realize I'm starting to get maudlin; sometimes this weather does it to you. It'll just sneak right up next to you, tap you on the head, and make you depressed. Like a magic trick.

I resolve to go find my brother and Zeb. Once I find them I'll feel better.

But there is something strange.

I don't know how to tell you this.

So, when I turn the corner, from under the colonnade down to the steps, there's a view from here over the particularly insane black-and-white-bottomed pool surrounded by Roman architecture. As if you just happened to step into ancient Rome at the height of the empire. Except not. Except half the world away in a place that's now just a museum and testament to a rich man's folly. But there, standing near the pool, leaning against a white Doric column—is Binky.

Of course she's crying. I bet you could fill that entire pool with just the tears out of her waylaid bride's eyes. She turns back, and I duck down behind a column because I am not insane, are you kidding me? How awkward would that be? "Hi, um, sorry about your wedding getting ruined by a bedraggled stranger." No. I am not doing it. As she turns back . . . she stares out over the Romanesque pool. Vacant. Like nobody's home. And this is a feeling I can understand.

I want to say something to her. To make it better.

But what would I say?

What would I do? Offer her a gift card to Target?

What am I even talking about?

Poor Binky.

This is just the worst day of her life.

I should go console her.

Okay, fine.

I'll do it.

Welcome to my world of awkwardness.

6

I TRY TO make my way down to Binky but manage to slip and nearly kill myself. I guess these rain-drizzled colonnades get pretty slick. I save myself with the world's most uncoordinated gesture and I can only hope Binky doesn't notice my ridiculous body spasm. My words of consolation won't work after that.

But when I look up, she's still in her own little world. Staring down at her hands, at her engagement ring. Her shoulders shake ever so slightly in her butterfly-sleeve Russian lace. Still crying. Alone in the rain on her wedding day, not even a coat on her shoulders. I guess she doesn't even care at this point. Maybe it's like, "Well, I threw the biggest wedding of all time, it was a fiasco and now I don't care if I get pneumonia and die." I mean, sure. And, let's be honest. This wedding really must have cost a fortune.

Maybe I've been too judgmental of Binky. Maybe something about her perfect everything was annoying to me. Maybe I was being protective of Zeb. Maybe I didn't give her a fair shot.

I will help her. I will stop being so selfish, insecure, and weird, and step right up to the plate. Put my big-girl pants on and march down there and make this woman feel better, right now!

Suddenly, I'm ashamed of myself. How selfish am I? My mother would not be proud of me for hesitating. She would get that look on her face of sad disappointment that would absolutely break my soul. She gave me that look once when I didn't want to give away my Duplo Legos even though I hadn't even looked at them for five years. "But, honey, some other little girl could play with them. Someone who didn't have any toys." I can feel my cheeks flush just thinking about it.

Okay, okay, no more funny business. I will go over there and make the bride feel better right this minute!

I resolve to be the best person I can be, exhale, and march down there, but it's too late, she's already heading back inside, probably to clean up her tears and be a good hostess. I catch one last glimpse of her, through the doorway, her makeup melted with tears.

Okay, I blew that.

I'll make up for it later.

Maybe a flower arrangement?

A handwritten, heartfelt note in a card?

But this train of thought is interrupted. Across the lawn I see Henry and Zeb rushing through the rain to the south entrance. I can only assume they have reached the finale of their adventure and are going inside to warm up and eat whatever catering you're supposed to eat at this point of a tragedy.

SSCCCCCHHHH.

Wait. What was that?

SSCCHCCC. SCCCHHHHH.

Um. What is happening right now?

I turn around to figure out where this strange noise is coming from and what it might be. By the sound of it, it's a dragon mixed with a television set.

I tiptoe backward, images of my robot–Jurassic Park end floating through my head. Yes, I will be eaten. The thing will swoop me up. The teeth will be metal antennas. The eyes will be screens!

But as I reach the back of the colonnade, I begin to recognize the sound. It's a security sound. A cop sound. The sound they make on their headsets or walkie-talkies or whatever those things are called.

SSCCCCHHHH.

SSSSSCCCCHHHHHHHHHH.

And then, I hear a man's voice picking up. It's hard to hear him over the scramble of the hand radio and the dribble drabble of the rain. But it's definitely a security guard's voice. Deep. Indifferent. On the job.

Strange that Henry and Zeb would go inside before they

rounded up *all* the guards. I mean, wasn't that their whole job description?

I peek out over the corner and, yep, just as I suspected. Security guard. Blue uniform. Matching hat. Black work shoes. Company insignia on the breast pocket. Check, check, check.

I'm just about to open my mouth and tell him what happened and how he has to get down the hill, like, yesterday, when I'm so rudely interrupted.

SSCHHHHHHH. "You there?"

"Yeah, I'm here."

See, just like I said. Security-guy talk.

And just before I'm about to plop myself smack-dab in the middle of this security-guy talk I hear it.

That same security-guy voice, coming through the speaker.

"Are they gone yet? I need you to tell me if the coast is clear."

Coast? Clear?

That doesn't sound like security-guy talk. That's *bad-guy talk.*

Which means I, your friend, Eva, am trapped in the pool-adjacent area . . . *with a bad guy.*

7

THERE ARE NOT many words to describe the feeling I have in this moment. But I'll start with panic.

Followed by—

Betrayal.

Fear.

Shock.

Disbelief.

Shock again.

Back to fear.

Annnnnd . . . panic.

As if all of a sudden the entire world turned inside out, and then turned itself into a chicken.

But a really bad chicken.

A devastating bit of poultry.

So, here I am, sitting here, on the other side of the colonnade, just steps away from . . . whoever these guys are. (Besides bad guys.) And what they might want.

"Are they gone yet?"

Are *they* gone? Are *who* gone? And why is there a *yet*? What exactly is the *yet* for? The *yet* implies a time issue. It implies that time is running out. *What will happen at that time?*

I don't want to know.

And yet, I have to know. Of course I have to know.

I freeze behind the corner and try to listen in. The rain is coming down harder, now in swooshes. *Swoosh. Swoosh. Swoosh.*

"Well, are they?"

"Hard to tell. I think so." That's the guy from my side. No static.

"Well, are they or aren't they?" That's coming over the airwaves. I can hear it. A kind of nasal, annoyed voice. American but not from here somehow. Not a California voice. No breeze in it. From a harder place.

He continues, "Jesus. Who the hell hired you for this job anyway? Dipstick!"

This *job*.

Okay, this is a job. A job that they are all doing together. Which I'm pretty sure at this point has nothing to do with security.

"You don't have to call me names. That's unprofessional."

"Unprofessional! Look, idiot, all I need you to do is take

your dumb eyes and put them on the dumb driveway and tell me if they're all gone or what?!"

"Well, it looks like all the guys are gone, but there were these two kids running around for a while."

Wait. He's talking about Henry and Zeb. Oh my god.

"Yeah, how old?"

"I dunno. Kids."

And now the guy on the other side is straining to be patient. "Kids like teenagers or kids like hey-Mom-read-me-a-bedtime-story?"

My guy thinks. "Not like hey-Mom-read-me-a-bedtime-story but maybe like hey-Dad-let's-go-play-catch."

Pause.

"What the heck is the difference?!" The guy on the other side is losing it.

"I'm just saying those are two very different stages of life. Unless, of course, the kid is really attached to his mom, which probably happens more and more these days—"

"Jesus! What are you even saying? Just tell me. Did they look like ten or what?"

"Maybe."

"MAYBE?! God, would you just?! Okay, let me put it like this. Are these the kind of kids who would be watching *Sponge-Bob* or *The Simpsons*?"

"Well, *The Simpsons* is really intergenerational so—"

"SWEET JESUS! Okay, were these the kind of kids who

would be watching *SpongeBob*?"

"Well, they looked a little old for *SpongeBob*."

"Okay, so ten. Ten or twelve. Yeah?"

"I think so . . . I mean, does it really matter what they watch?"

"Yes. Yes, dillweed, it does matter. Because what they watch, or what they read, which I can't ask you because you've never read a book in your life, is an indication of how old they are and how old they are is an indication of whether or not they can foil our plan. Got it, genius?"

"Yeah. Okay, yeah. I get it now."

"Thank you. Now let's try again—"

"You don't have to worry, boss."

"Oh, and why is that?"

"These kids look kinda wimpy."

"How wimpy?"

"On a scale of one to ten . . . like a hundred."

"Okay, good. So we don't have to take them out?"

"Oh, no. No way. Total wimps."

"Okay, good. Now get back here for phase two. Don't let anybody see you, especially those kids. You hear me?"

"Yeah, yeah, I hear you."

And now the guy nearest to me packs it up. With an exhale, he shuffles off down the steps in the other direction, leaving me to try to put *that* whole conversation in order.

Take them out.

I mean . . . *take them out*?

Really?

All I can say is, I have never, in my entire life, been more thankful that my kid brother, and his friend, come across as so heavily, obviously, undeniably . . . unthreatening.

8

THIS IS MY first wedding and, suffice to say, I do not want it to be the last. Not least of which because I don't think this wedding is providing me with a good window into what weddings are like in general.

There is one thing for sure. I have to, this second, before one more millisecond goes by, go, get, grab Henry and tell him about the diabolical machinations of this fallen matrimony. Someone/someones are *pulling a job* here at this grand event!

I'm still trying to figure out if I should tell Zeb. I mean, it might be really disappointing for him, since it *is* his dad's wedding and all, plus there is the undeniable possibility that everyone will think I'm crazy, so that will be fun. "Greetings, wedding guests! Bad news! We're being trapped here by a band of wild criminals!" I mean, would you ever believe that?

Now that I think about it, though, the idea of a band of criminals "taking over" a town, albeit a miniscule one, also seems sort of far-fetched. But the story got more than half of the adults at this wedding to up and leave!

I mean, does it make more sense that perhaps that was just a ridiculous ruse to get all the able-bodied folks to put on their hero hats and rush downhill to save the day? I don't have time to ponder that now. I'll ponder that later. Over a cup of tea in a study somewhere. For right now—Henry.

And that's when the sky opens up.

Cats and dogs. Cows and chickens.

I mean, this is almost a typhoon.

Remember, last time this happened a huge section of the PCH was taken out and an entire new shoreline was created! So . . . not good. The roads will definitely be closed. Which means that whatever the impromptu posse finds down there at the bottom of the cliff, thirteen miles up the PCH, it may not matter. Because by the time they find out, they will not be able to get back *here*. Where there is *actual visual and auditory confirmation* of criminal activity!

And the rain continues to pour down from the sky.

You may be wondering if I plan on just staying out here in this deluge. Well, dear friend, I think you know me better than that by now. I am sensible. I've found a little alcove to slip into, here on what must be the fortieth landing of this baroque castle. This would be an epic place to pay hide-and-seek, by the way.

Henry would never find me.

There's a little arched window with diagonal panes, each like diamonds, like there should be a dragon somewhere around. I look in and realize it actually stands above the chapel, aka the place where the wedding was taking place before disaster struck. The guests down there are sitting around, but they don't look bored or impatient exactly.

Strange.

Why wouldn't they just adjourn to the reception area and try to make the best of it? It's clear the wedding's not happening. Might as well take advantage of the vittles and libations. But there's something else. They look nervous. Every once in a while, I see one of them cast a fleeting glance at another and then look away.

And then I see it.

What in the Sam Hill?

Okay, I need to take a breath while I process this. Breathe. Breathe, Eva. Slow down. Get ahold of yourself. Okay.

So, what's happening is . . . the entirety of the wedding is sitting there, in the chapel, in their formalwear, shaken, while at the perimeter of the chapel, in each of the four arched doorways, stands a man in heavy security garb. Yep, ladies and germs, these guys are holding the entire room hostage.

But why?

I mean who in the world holds an entire wedding hostage?

But then it hits me: We are in the biggest depository of precious art on the west coast—or even maybe both coasts. This place, Hearst Castle, must be filled with millions of dollars' worth of art. Maybe even a billion. So, they had hired security for the wedding. That was part of the deal. But, clearly, the security they hired is not the security they got.

What they got was a gang of robbers in disguise.

I'm just about to contemplate what to do next when the unthinkable happens. I look down at the left back entrance, near the holy water, and see both Henry and Zeb being ushered in by one of these security brutes.

Ushered is putting it gently. They basically just push them into the room and point to the rest of the group, to take a seat.

Zeb takes a seat and puts his arm around a septuagenarian woman who looks extremely upset, comforting her. Maybe she's his great-aunt or something?

But not Henry. I look at Henry and know exactly what is going on.

The wheels are turning.

He's already put all of this together.

And he's figuring out a way out of it.

9

I HAVE TO wonder if this isn't all some elaborate party setup, like a Murder Mystery Wedding, or some dinner-theater thing we went to once where the actors were also the waiters. Very disorienting. I remember being disappointed our waiter wasn't one of the leads. Just a minor character asking if we wanted a baked potato or fries.

That would be the perfect explanation, wouldn't it?

But it wouldn't explain why Binky was crying, or why half of the guests were sent away.

The guests that are left are being guarded. But if I'm honest, it's a relaxed kind of monitoring. It's as though these criminals, or art thieves, or wedding crashers, are just assuming the women and elderly left in the chapel can't *do* anything. I mean, have they ever met a woman before?

There's a dark medieval-looking door across the alcove I can make it to, if I duck so no one sees me through the window. Not that anybody seems to be looking up here, but better safe than sorry. I'm just hoping it isn't locked, that these "security guards" left everything open to make their epic thievery that much easier.

I duck under the arched window and find myself in some kind of parlor. A sitting room of sorts? Or, if I were in any other place . . . a ballroom. The wallpaper is a kind of teal damask and there's gold molding in a line near the top of the fifteen-foot ceiling. Also, the ceiling. There's a mural on that ceiling, which is mostly black and white, gilded in shades of gold. There's a giant painting in the middle, and then a series of little, also gold-gilded, paintings around it. I'm sort of breaking my neck trying to discern what exactly is being depicted here, but that doesn't matter because while I'm taking it all in I back into the enormous gray stone fireplace.

Yes, I am now standing *inside* the fireplace, it's that big. But that doesn't matter, either, because as I look up at the ceiling from my little cove in the fireplace, I realize that the figures in the painting are . . . they're *moving*. Swirling in and out of the gold-gilded picture frame. Yes, they're coming to life and emerging from their frames.

And moving toward me.

10

THERE'S NOTHING WORSE than being stuck in an enormous stone fireplace with paintings flying at you. Or people from paintings. Or two-dimensional representations of people. But here we are.

As the figures come closer they begin to morph into something less High Renaissance and more low American. Especially the first one . . . Beaumont.

Now, as I mentioned briefly before, Henry and I became acquainted with a few of our ancestors almost a year ago. And I don't mean we read about them. I mean they showed up. In ghost form. All five of them.

If you don't remember, I'll give you the broad strokes.

Great-great-great-great-grandfather Beaumont. Gold miner.

Founder of the family fortune in the 1849 gold rush. Overalls. Corncob pipe. (Which is what eventually killed him, by the way. Ahem. Smoking is stupid.)

Then there is his wife, our great-great-great-great-grandmother Plum. Stout. Loving. Sensible. Victorian dress and ever-present lace fan. She's the one that kind of comes across as warm milk and cookies.

Then there are the two sophisticated twins, August and Sturdevant, dandies of the roaring twenties. The grandsons of Beaumont. And our great-uncles, I suppose. They lived in tandem and died in tandem, in a convertible Model A car crash in Rome. See, even their death was sophisticated.

And then there was Maxine. The morose, melancholy flapper. We think she just died of gloom.

But whatever the case may be, somehow these renaissance paintings have floated down from the ceiling, through the ether, and metamorphosed into our darling, most dear ancestor ghosts.

Startling, yes.

Also kind of cool.

"Hey, there, little filly! Seems you got yourself in a real pickle here!"

No matter how many times they materialize, my ancestors' actual appearance always results in a racing heart and a dry throat. It's the effect the supernatural has on the living.

It takes me a moment to regain myself.

"I . . . you . . ."

"Don't worry, darlin'. Hope we didn't scare ya, poppin' out of the pictures like that! The boys here wanted to show off!" Beauregard gestures to August and Sturdy.

"Quite right, quite right." They clink martini glasses, proud of their expert ghosting.

Maxine slumps toward them. "Couldn't you have chosen something a little less gaudy for us to make our appearance? All this gold. Gold gold gold! As if life was more than a walking shadow—"

"Aw, jeez. There she goes! What did I make all this money for if you're all just gonna slump around groaning?!"

Plum turns to me, changing the subject. "Oh, dearest Eva. I'm afraid we've been summoned again. There's trouble afoot."

"I'll say," I answer. "Did you see those guys in there? Wait a minute, how can you even be here? I mean, we're like miles away from our house. Where your graves are. How are you able to get this much range when I can't even get a signal on my cell phone?"

"Oh, honey, there is so much to understand, and so little time, but we have years of experience ghosting. Years and years of practice—"

"Yep, we can follow you anywhere! London! Tokyo! Bombay! Heck, we'd follow you to the moon if we had to! We are sworn to protect our kin, and dagnabbit, that's what we're gonna do. Rain or shine!" Beau smokes his corncob pipe, the smoke wafting up through his translucent body.

Plum comes forward, confidentially. "To tell you the truth

though, August and Sturdy used to practically live here."

"Indeed, indeed." They nod in tandem.

Plum adds, "And Maxine came here once."

"It was a bore." She sighs.

"Can you beat that? Man builds a real-life wonder here and this little filly calls it a bore! Well, excuuuuse me while I just paint Mars green for you, your ladyship!"

"I'm just saying it was tedious," Maxine laments.

"Tedious, shmedious!" Beau snaps.

We're clearly getting off track. "Look. You're right. Your kin, aka me and Henry, are in serious trouble and I don't know what to do. You have to help me. Henry's down there!"

"Don't I know it! Whattaya think we're here for!" Beaumont exclaims.

"Indubitably, indubitably." August and Sturdy nod.

Maxine moans, "Aren't we just staving off the inevitable, pretending there is hope, when, indeed, there can never be—"

"Oh, quit it! We got lives to save! Eva, little darlin', it's up to you!" Beaumont steps in closer. "Boop!" He dabs me right smack on the tip of my nose.

"Up to *me*?" I shrink.

"Yes, dear child. We know you're up to the challenge. Your brother, Henry, needs you. As do the rest." Plum breaks the news, her words fuzzy and kind.

"Undoubtedly, unquestionably," August and Sturdy aver.

Plum moves forward now. "This is a place of spirits, Evie.

Myriad spirits. So many voices from the past. Echoing. Some wise, some restless."

"Quite, quite," August and Sturdy add.

"And yer gonna get 'em!" Beaumont nods.

"Um . . . *get* them?" I gulp.

"Yup, yer gonna snatch 'em right out of the woodwork so you can outsmart these bandits! You'll see. Works like a charm. Well, come to think of it, it is a charm."

"I'm sorry . . . I'm confused."

Plum moves closer to me. "The spirits are here, Eva. You simply have to reach them. They will come to your aid."

"But how?" I ask.

And now the ghosts are fading, disappearing back into the ether and back up into the paintings, as if nothing happened and this is all just a hallucination of a panicked child.

"Underneeeeath the chapel, Evaaaa," Maxine lilts, the last one to fade. "Uuuuunder the chaaaapel."

And now I am left, a stone in a stone fireplace, wondering if it's possible I'm just losing my mind.

"That can't happen. Did that just happen?" I turn to a white marble bust of Tiberius Caesar next to me on a pedestal, staring out, the grave conqueror.

He doesn't answer.

But I've been through this before, and the truth is—it's always in your best interest to do what the ghosts say.

PART TWO

1

HAVE YOU EVER had so many things to do that you just feel like running under the covers and never coming out? Like all the things in the world just add up to this gigantic worry monster that you can only fend off by pulling the covers over your head? That's how I feel right now. I don't even know where to start.

First, there's the imminent danger below in the chapel. Then, there's the mystery *underneath* the chapel, that might somehow help me with what's going on *inside* the chapel, but maybe not . . . ugh.

I don't know what I'm supposed to do first. I mean, this is not exactly what they teach in school these days. Prioritizing spirit-calling and Confusing Castle Situations 101.

Okay. Okay.

Maybe, I think, if I can just figure out a way to get to Henry, he and I can do this together. Two heads are better than one, right? So, um, now just to figure out a way to get his attention without also getting the attention of those horrible-daunting-terrifying-looking guys scowling at each doorway.

It's on me. It's on me.

All right, think. Think, Eva.

I know. I'll create a distraction.

A distraction!

These guys don't look like the brightest bulbs in the dashboard.

What is the most distracting thing I can do that's easy to accomplish, but will be large enough to give me enough time to get Henry's attention? See, if I were Henry, I would probably have a million chemical experiments in my back pocket just to throw out the way most people can rattle off the alphabet.

But I'm not Henry. And I need Henry.

So let's just keep it simple, shall we?

Fire.

Yes, fire.

Kids, do not try this at home.

FROM WHERE I'M squinting, looking down below, Henry and Zeb are at one end of the chapel, with two guards near them and two at the other end. So, I'm going to have to get everyone to go to the far end, while making sure Henry and Zeb stay on their end.

Okay, okay. I'll start a little teeny tiny fire on the other end, tiptoe over to their end, yell "Fire!" from behind those red velvet curtains, and then grab Henry before he can run over to the now not-so-teeny fire distraction event.

The giant stone fireplace next to me has a long, oval-shaped, rose-printed container next to me, which I'm pretty sure houses the matches for the fireplace. Okay, grab that. Grab that fire stoking thing. (What is it called? A poker? That seems like a pretty lazy name, actually. I mean, couldn't they come up with something a little more wizardly? Like a hoffenpoffer.) It's a black wrought-iron thing, possibly useful in a fight against . . . whoever these guys are.

As I tiptoe out to hatch my diabolical plan, I hear the sound of footsteps coming down the hall toward me, a hollow sound, echoing off the marble floors. And now voices, one of them familiar, the nonCalifornia, Midwestern-sounding voice.

"What did I tell you? Leave the rugs! I'm not looking to open a rug store, for God's sake!"

I duck behind the teal floor-to-ceiling curtains behind me, hoping to catch even a glimpse of this always-agitated criminal . . . mastermind?

"Look, we don't have much time, get it? If the rain stops, they'll open the road back up. If the rain keeps going, we'll get stuck in the mud! . . . I don't care what they're worth. No rugs! They're cumbersome . . ."

"What does—"

"Oh my God, cumbersome! Slow! They take a long time, okay? Just stop what you're doing and listen to me. Paintings first, then statues, then— Hold on a second."

The footsteps stop. The voice stops.

On the other end I can hear the sound of a voice, but the Midwestern Mastermind interrupts him.

"Shh. Shut up. Shut all the way up."

And now he begins slowly walking backward, retracing his steps, back to the doorway of *this room*.

He's walking softer now, as if trying to catch someone. Quiet.

I'm a statue behind the teal drapes, holding my breath, hoping to God my shoes aren't sticking out of the bottom of the curtains but too scared to look down, not wanting to shake the velvet.

The Midwestern Mastermind peeks his head into the room. looking around. He comes in slightly, taking in the paintings and the ceiling. But his neck is up, suspicious.

Static comes over the line of his walkie-talkie.

"You there, boss?"

"Shh." He looks around some more, as if there's something here he senses, a presence. He spends an inordinate amount of time looking at the ceiling.

And then he looks directly—at me.

3

HAVE YOU EVER had one of those dreams where you're at the grocery store or the park or your school and suddenly you look down and realize you're completely naked? One hundred percent in your birthday suit. And the embarrassment and fear are almost overwhelming. Like you want to run away but you are just paralyzed with fear and confusion so you just stand there, a buck-naked statue in the middle of the cafeteria?

Welp, that's the feeling that I'm having now. Minus the embarrassed part. Standing there behind the velvet floor to ceilings with grumpy-yet-diabolical Mastermind of the Hearst Castle Heist in the middle of the room, staring directly at me. Or through me. Can he see me? How long can I hold my breath? Seriously, my record is two minutes. Not bad, but I used to be on swim team and you had to be able to swim to the other end of the pool and back holding your breath. But I'm out of practice. So I'm guessing more like one minute?

And this is taking a thousand years.

The Midwestern Mastermind starts to squint a little, taking one step closer, as if his spider sense is on full tilt.

And now one step closer.

And another.

And one more.

So, I'd say he's about . . . um, four-five feet away from me right now?

Gulp.

Basically, what's going to happen is he's going to jump forward, catch me, drag me downstairs, and throw me to the wolves in front of everyone to make an example of me. Not that I saw any wolves or anything. These are metaphorical wolves. But here, definitely gold ones. From the Egyptian dynasty.

I've somehow lost my train of thought and have begun wondering if wolves were even depicted by the Egyptians in any hieroglyphs, considering their predilection for, fascination with, and adoration of cats. And all things feline. I mean you couldn't swing a dead cat in Ancient Egypt without running into a hieroglyph of . . . a cat. Bad joke, I know. But you have to admit . . . pretty clever under the circumstances.

I would almost smile, if the situation here wasn't so dire. I mean, who knows, it might be my last smile. My last great stand against the Midwestern Mastermind and his invading army of fake security guards. Laughter in the face of fear. Joy in the face of hopelessness. They will build statues of me now, statues of my noble smile amid the chaos of the fall of Hearst Castle. A plaque underneath me, engraved in gold, will read:

"In honor of Eva Millicent Billings. Despite the madness, she smiled."

Okay, that's horrible.

How about:

"In honor of the deceased, Eva Millicent Billings. A true hero, who never allowed . . . the turkeys to get her down"?

What am I talking about?

I'm really losing my mind here.

Maybe this is what happens when you're about to go? You just get silly. Maybe the meaninglessness of it all just comes to you. All the struggles of the world, all the plans, maybe they come bounding down at you right before the moment of death, and you could laugh, you could cry laughing, at all the wasted effort put into, say, that test you crammed for until all hours of the night. Maybe the futileness of it all comes hurtling at you like a weight. And then a weight lifted. Ah! None of it mattered all along! Nobody told me! It was all for naught!

(I'm beginning to sound like Maxine.)

(I'm beginning to understand Maxine.)

Wait. Maybe it's in my blood?

SCCCCRRRCTHHHHC. SCCRRTCH. SCCRRTCH.

The static interrupts my melancholy revelation and the Midwestern Mastermind jumps where he is.

"GEEZ!"

"Boss, you there?"

"Stop doing that! You know what, I'm turning off this thing unless I contact *you*! Got it? I contact you. You do *not* contact me. I'm turning this stupid thing off. And, yes, I'm here, dipstick. Where do you think I'd be?!"

"I just. Was wondering. Awful quiet. Oh, I forgot what I was gonna tell you. . . . Oh, yeah, those kids are gone."

"What?"

"'Member those two kids?"

"Which kids?"

"The wimpy ones?"

"Yes." The Midwestern Mastermind rolls his eyes.

"Wull, they escaped kinda."

"What? What do you mean they escaped *kinda*? Did they escape or what?" Now the Midwestern Mastermind face-palms, sitting down on the chinoiserie silk chaise lounge, dark blue and gold birds nestled in branches.

"Wull, they got out."

"They got out where? Where did they get to?"

"I dunno, there was just a commotion on one side of the room and then, next thing we know, they were just, I dunno. Gone, I guess."

"You guess! You guess? You nincompoop!"

So, Henry and Zeb executed *my* plan! They created a distraction on one side of the room and then bailed out the other. I love it. Great minds think alike!

Again, I would smile, but the dark lord Mastermind is face-palming right there in front of me.

"Lookit. You find those little trolls and bring them back to me. I've had just about enough of this *Paw Patrol* nonsense! I am not going to be foiled by a bunch of kindergarteners!"

Beat.

"I really don't think they're in kindergarten."

"Jesus, Mary, and Joseph! Get me those kids before I—"

"Okay, boss."

The Midwestern Mastermind stands up in frustration, chucking his walkie-talkie past me and into a Ming dynasty vase five feet to my left.

CRASH.

"AAHHHHHHHH!"

It is clear that the Midwestern Mastermind is not having a good day. Suffice to say the only one having a worse day is Binky. At least for the Mastermind, it wasn't supposed to be his wedding day.

Although, to be honest, I'm not sure the Midwestern Mastermind could get anyone to actually marry him. He's kind of skinny as a straw and has a face like a gravel driveway. I mean, my mother said never to judge, and she's right, but this guy looks as mean and frustrated on the outside as he is on the inside, like his whole existence is just a scrunched-up mistake where nothing ever goes right. Dark circles under his eyes like he's been up since 2003.

But he's not out of the room yet.

He stomps over, swooping up his walkie-talkie in one hand and storming out, not looking back.

Phew.

That was a close one.

Now, to get to my brother.

4

I'VE GOT SOME good news and some bad news.

The good news is that the Midwestern Mastermind, aka MM, has disappeared. The bad news is that all of this is still happening and isn't just some bad dream I'm having. I keep pinching myself to see if maybe I just fell asleep during "Pachelbel's Canon," but every time I just come up with some red skin and a renewed sense of panic.

It's clear from the overheard phone call that the first thing on my agenda has to be finding Henry. And Zeb. Before this menagerie of faux guards finds them and brings them to the Machiavellian Midwestern Mastermind. Triple M.

Now, let's see, how to do this?

In order to find Henry, I have to try to think like Henry.

What would Henry do? If I were Henry and I escaped from the chapel of confined guests and lunkhead guards, what would be the first thing I'd do?

I know!

Find Eva!

(Aka me.)

And if I were me, where would I go? Or, wait, if I were Henry thinking about me, where would he think I would go? Hmmm. Think, Eva. Did I express interest in any particular things before the great wedding disturbance? Was there anything I said I was looking forward to seeing? An area of interest, perhaps?

Wait.

The bloodthirsty protector of Ra! The sun god. The New Kingdom Egyptian statues! That's what we were talking about before the great wedding debacle.

But would Henry go there? Thinking that I was there?

My head hurts.

Just go to the Egyptian statues, I tell myself.

Tiptoeing through a labyrinth of corridors, alcoves, and sitting rooms, I can catch a glimpse, every once in a while, of the inside of the chapel below. Even though there are menacing guards, I find it hard to believe the remaining wedding guests are all just going to sit around for this whole shebang. Maybe in Victorian times, but now? Really?

There is the issue of the weather, however. What was it the Midwestern Mastermind was saying? The roads are closed because of the rain. But if the roads open up, I'm pretty sure all the heroes that rode downhill on their white stallions will be back. And not happy.

But if it keeps pouring like this, I have a hard time imagining truckload after truckload after truckload of paintings, precious jewels, and sculptures heading down the steep incline toward the sea and not getting stuck.

So the clock is ticking.

But the clock is also ticking on Henry and Zeb. I mean, you heard the diabolical Mastermind. He said bring them back to him. And in the first conversation, he asked his henchman if he should *take them out*.

Take them out where?

(I don't think he means to the store.)

Now, if I can just find the two Sekhmet figures, the blood-thirsty protectors of the sun god, maybe, possibly, potentially Henry will be there because he was trying to think like I would think.

Let's all agree that it's complicated.

But at this point, it's really all I have, and I'm sort of desperate to find Henry. He is my kid brother, after all. Even if he is a budding Einstein.

I'm at about a half run–half tiptoe down the servant's stairwell when I hear a sound coming from within the hall. The sound of the wedding guests raising their voices. Then a few unreasonable, bullying voices barking orders back.

I suppose the menacing guards are trained at keeping masses

of unsuspecting people under control. Unsuspecting wedding guests.

I shake my head.

You have to admit.

It's a dirty trick.

When I find Henry, we'll need to find a way to be dirty trickier.

5

WHEN WE WERE little, before "the accident" (which is what we still call the death of our mother and father. Not the "boat sinking," not "the explosion," and certainly not "the murder." It's just "the accident." It has to be that way. It was an unwritten agreement between Henry and me. Never spoken of. Never discussed.

Once the mystery was solved and our traitor hippie uncle Finn was put in jail, Henry and I had to brace ourselves with words like "the accident" and "passing."

Gentle words. Kind words. Words you could carry off on a butterfly's wings. Not words that could sink you to the bottom of the sea forever. Never. Never those words.)

There was a vacation, a Thanksgiving, I think, when we went to visit our uncle Claude in what they call the "hill country" of Texas. A strange sort of place, nestled right in the middle of the Lone Star State. I always thought Texas looked like that super-old movie *Giant* with James Dean squinting into an oil rig, but I guess that's just one part. Turns out there's five parts of Texas. The desert. The hill country. The plains up north. The "big thicket" of pines to the east. And the swamp, which is the Gulf Coast part that always gets the hurricanes.

But in this case we were smack-dab in the middle of the hill country at Uncle Claude's ranch, which was more like a church to dead animals. I mean it, you've never seen such a collection of noble and gallant creatures, all now stuffed and posed in some ridiculous fashion imitating life, in a house in Texas under a cathedral ceiling. A lion about to pounce on a gazelle. A leopard on its hind legs. A wildebeest drinking from a bubbling fountain. Somebody really put some thought and effort into this taxidermy menagerie. And it was awful.

Henry took one look at it and started crying. He was five. He's always been what we call "sensitive." I think it's something about all those neurons buzzing around in his brain, like he can pick up the signals of all God's creatures. Feel for them. Empathize with them. Just be in their place. Just be them.

And in that moment, the moment of seeing the menagerie of killed animals, it was as if Henry experienced the pain and sadness of not just the animals before us, but the animals left behind. The mother cub, the pack, the baby gazelle now orphaned.

And I remember Uncle Claude being confused by this little display. Dumbfounded. He actually thought "the kids" would love it. Like we'd think it was a sort of zoo-meets-museum and climb aboard. He had no idea who he was dealing with. Just like he had no idea who he was dealing with later when he asked if Henry wanted to come out and wait in a blind all day while he was going to shoot deer.

Shoot. Deer.

I mean, first of all, Henry. And second of all, Henry would never do anything to a deer except maybe try to make friends with it by using a soft calming voice and an app he specially designed to speak Deerish, or whatever you want to call their particular language.

So, that was a hard no on shooting deer.

But I remember the way Uncle Claude and his friends got all gussied up for the shooting—uh, *hunting*. In camo outfits and funny hats. As if it mattered. I mean, they were just going to be sitting in a blind, which, true to its name, like obscures everything about you from sight. The way they were dressed, you'd think these guys were going to liberate a country. But nope, just sitting in a tin box sort of suspended in the air, waiting for the poor deer to come by and eat the deer food laid out for them. Then shoot them.

Pretty noble.

My mother and father just sat there on the back deck,

squiggly mouth smiles on both of them. It's a relief that Henry had no desire to go, because cats would have sprouted wings before my mother let that happen. Dogs would have jumped over the moon.

But here, on my way down to the New Kingdom Egyptian statues, I listen to the sounds of the guards raising their voices, some kind of a struggle, a loud crash, and then more pandemonium. And I hope to God Henry and Zeb aren't sitting ducks underneath a blind.

6

THE PROTECTOR OF the sun god statues are supposed to be facing out over the gardens, which is exactly the opposite of where I am. The only direct way is straight through the castle, and I think we all know that's a really bad idea.

So, again, it's back to navigating this maze while walking on eggshells, trying not to get caught by the Midwestern Mastermind and his dastardly crew of illiterate guards.

I am managing just fine, slithering my way through the servants' quarters, downstairs from all the commotion, when I look over and see, through a tiny window, a row of trucks like an army battalion being loaded in with precious art. Said art, FYI, is being handled the way most people would treat a potato sack. I mean, are these guys mindless or what? What good is it to steal irreplaceable artifacts and bazillion-dollar paintings if you break them apart on the way?

Apparently, I'm not the only one who feels that way, because despite the driving rain I see the Midwestern Mastermind's skinny, hunched-over body come barreling out of the side entrance, gesticulating wildly with his hands. I have a pretty good idea what he's saying, and I bet if he were in school he'd get in trouble for some of his word choices.

The minions just stand there, taking in his harangue and nodding, until he gives them a final piece of mind and storms away. At which point, they all look at one another and shrug, then go back to doing it the exact same way.

Poor Midwestern Mastermind.

He should have hired some more artistically inclined criminals. French criminals, for instance. Or Italian ones. Now, that would make the whole thing much more chic! But no, he hired Tweedledee and Tweedledumber and the rest of their tweedly crew.

Poor Midwestern Mastermind? What am I talking about? The Midwestern Mastermind is the one trying to "take out" my kid brother and his new BFF. I must be losing my mind in all this chaos. They'll find me one day in the attic of the castle, my hair wild and frazzled, missing teeth, with a thousand cats who I've all named RumpleMeowskins. RumpleMeowskins Number One. RumpleMeowskins Number Two . . . all the way up to a thousand. I will survive on a diet of berries and rainwater.

By the time I actually make my way down to the Egyptian statues, the rain is coming down in buckets again. As if the angels themselves are just gleefully throwing down pail after pail of water from the heavens, mad with holy power. I debate whether to stand right next to the statues or to stand nearby.

Pros of standing next to the statues: Can be seen by Henry. Cons of standing next to the statues: Can be seen by the Midwestern Mastermind and his motley crew.

Okay, the best thing to do is stand nearby and look for a sign. But what if Henry and Zeb are standing by looking for a sign? And then we are all just hiding, standing around looking for a sign and not seeing one another.

I know. A bird sound.

A bird sound is definitely in order.

"KAW-KAW!"

The sound throws itself out into the rain, muddled by all the raindrops.

I sit there, waiting for a reply. . . .

Nothing.

Okay, maybe a different bird. Like an eagle.

"KAH-wa-wa-wa. KAH-wa-wa-wa."

Okay, my eagle call definitely leaves something to be desired. I resolve to work on it.

I listen, waiting for the reply.

Again, nothing.

Sigh. What am I thinking? Henry is clearly waiting for a more obvious sign. I need a bird that's not indigenous to the

Northern California coastal area. One that will stick out in his mind.

Okay, what about a prairie warbler? That's distinctive. And Henry will know it's not an actual bird but a fake bird and, therefore, me. If you're wondering how we know all these bird sounds, see: Our dad. Environmentalists generally cannot get enough of nature, hikes, recognizing birds by their calls, and even recognizing animals by their "droppings." I know, gross.

Okay, let's try the prairie warbler, shall we? It's a little whistle that crescendos, getting fast, and then stops.

"Chirp. Chirp. Chirp chirp chirp chirp chirp."

I listen.

"Chirp. Chirp. Chirp chirp chirp chirp chirp."

And again.

Nothing.

Epic fail! They are not even here! Or anywhere around! And I am standing out here in the pouring rain whistling to myself like an idiot.

But then I hear it.

Across the gardens.

"Chirp. Chirp. Chirp chirp chirp chirp chirp."

Oh my God, it's him. It's Henry.

I chirp back.

"Chirp. Chirp. Chirp chirp chirp chirp chirp."

And now he chirps back, getting closer.

"Chirp. Chirp. Chirp chirp chirp chirp chirp."

I can see some rustling movements through the gardens, the

foliage swaying this way and that. I decide to quit chirping while they find me, as a safety precaution in case the criminals are nearby.

"Eva!" A whisper, elated. Henry peeks out of the foliage. "Oh, what a relief! We were quite worried."

And now Zeb peeks out from behind a shrub. "Whistle codes. I can't believe it. You guys are so cool."

Henry and I grab each other, hugging. Usually we avoid such displays but I think we can all agree there is nothing usual about today.

"Henry," I whisper during our hug, "I saw the ghosts!"

Henry frowns. "Which ghosts?"

But now the hug is done. So I try to talk out of the side of my mouth so Zeb can't hear. "You know, *our* ghosts?"

Zeb's mouth twists in confusion. "You guys have ghosts?"

Henry and I share a glance. Henry shrugs as if to say, *go ahead*.

I take a deep breath, then explain. "They're our ancestors. From the 1800s. We didn't go looking for them. They just kind of showed up. And kept showing up. At the weirdest times. They'd be kind of annoying if they weren't sort of hilarious."

Zeb turns to Henry. "Um, do you think maybe your sister drank the *adult* punch?"

But Henry steps forward. "Beaumont? And Plum? And—"

"Yes, yes, and August and Sturdy and even Maxine. All of them. They came out of the paintings on the ceiling and then morphed in front of me. It was August and Sturdy's idea and, apparently, they wanted a real showstopper."

Zeb looks at me, concerned. "Hold up. Are we talking *actual ghosts* here?"

Henry turns to him. "Yes. People who were once alive and now inhabit the spectral plane. I know it sounds crazy but—"

"There's no time to explain it now, Henry. We have to go! They said there are spirits all over this place. Spirits that will help us. Spirits that we can summon—"

"Okay, we're *summoning* spirits now. Maybe we could summon some aliens, too? Also some french fries, because I am starving," Zeb jokes.

"I'm serious, Zeb. Henry, we have to go under the chapel. That's where they said we'll find them."

"Underneath the chapel? Are there catacombs? A sarcophagus, possibly?"

"Whatever it is, we have to go!" I urge him.

Zeb steps forward. "Catacombs? Sarcophagi? I'm not exactly sure what is happening right now but I am *so* down with it. Let's go!"

Henry and I look at him.

Zeb is truly one of a kind.

"All right," Henry begins, "we have to determine how to get underneath the castle without alerting this band of criminals."

"I call them the tweedles. Because they're Tweedledee and

Tweedledumber. And they have a criminal mastermind telling them all what to do. A Midwestern mastermind. Sometimes I just call him MM."

"I love M&M's," Zeb says, wistfully.

Henry and I both look at him.

He shrugs. "What? I said I was hungry."

But Henry is already on his way. "Come on. There must be a back stairwell."

Zeb and I look at each other, following Henry through the maze of rosebushes, heading out toward the chapel in the rain. It hasn't let up. Good news and bad news.

Good news: This merry band of tweedles might get stuck in the mud. Bad news: the roads are still closed.

No one is coming to help. It's still up to us.

7

AFTER ABOUT TEN minutes of looking for a back entrance
to the chapel, Zeb sits down on a stone bench in front of a wall
of ivy. Henry and I are trying to decipher a tourist map of the
grounds but it's a faded one we grabbed out of the garbage, with
at least two coffee spills and about five crinkles. Still, better
than nothing.

"Look at this. So cool." Zeb is admiring an insignia on the
bench depicting Hades and a group of shrouded figures passing
over the river Styx, a grim reaper at the helm, his skull barely
perceptible behind his robe. "See, they've even engraved the
coins to pay for passage to the underworld."

"It's a triptych," Henry tells him, "showing each part of the
journey: real world, Styx, the underworld."

Henry and I rebury our heads in the map. Then we hear him.

"Uh, guys?"

"Zeb, we're kind of concentrating over here."

"Yeah, cool, but, guys?"

"Just a second." I try not to sound annoyed.

"All right, well, I kind of just touched these gold coins in this picture and then this wall just kind of, um, opened," Zeb says, cool as a cucumber.

Henry and I both look up from our map.

And, indeed, the ivy wall behind the bench has *opened up* to reveal what looks like a long and winding corridor into darkness.

Gulp.

"Sort of looks like it could go . . . under the chapel, yeah?" Zeb ponders.

"Uh, yeah." I look at Henry.

Henry beams like the sun. "Well done, *mon amie!*"

The three of us hesitate a bit at the foot of the entrance.

"We're all still really into this, right? Like we're totally gonna do this?" Zeb asks.

The air from the passageway is colder than the rest of the castle. It swirls around our ankles, seeming to pool there.

"Uhhh. Yeah," I mumble.

"N-no choice," Henry stutters. "This must be the way."

He steps into the opening. Zeb and I follow behind.

We tiptoe together into the passageway, then, about twenty

feet in, we hear the sound of something squeaking and then latching.

"What was that?" Henry turns.

Zeb takes a few steps back. Turns around.

"Uh. Well, I don't think we should panic or anything but, um . . . that viney secret-passageway door we went through . . . just closed."

8

AT THE NEWS of the closed passage behind us, Henry and I stand, frozen.

Zeb tries to make it better. "I do feel like there's a bright side here."

"And what is that?" I ask.

"Well, I mean, there could be like flying zombies in here, so, right there we're ahead of the game."

Flying zombies.

"And look—there's some light ahead." He jogs several feet in front of us and stops at a fixture casting a weak glow into its immediate vicinity. Several more line the wall of the corridor. "Sconces! I mean, without sconces it would be pitch-black in here. So I would definitely put that in the positive column," Zeb assures.

"He's right," Henry admits. "Let's think about this for a second. Our ancestor ghosts advised us to search here. Under the chapel. It's not logical they would send us into danger."

I think about it. "That's true. So, let's just keep going and see where this leads."

The passageway winds down in a swirl, farther and farther underground in a circular slope.

Zeb chuckles. "I kind of wish I had my skateboard."

Henry interrupts him. "Shh. Listen, above. Do you hear that, Eva?"

The three of us stop.

Up above we can hear the sound of the tweedle thugs barking out orders at the wedding guests, who are now technically hostages, but I can't bear to call them that.

"Lady, I said it once. Don't make me say it again. If you just calm down, stay still, you'll get out of here alive. Get it?" This is also not a California accent.

"How can we even hear them?" Zeb asks, craning his head upward.

"There must be some sort of ventilation system."

BANG.

The three of us freeze.

BANG. BANG.

All of us staring at one another.

We hear the frantic voices of the wedding guests. A commotion and a flurry of activity.

"Make sense now, ladies?" The tweedle speaks, puffed up on power.

Was that a . . . gun?

"We have to help them." I look at Henry.

"We *are* helping. Let's just hurry." Henry bounds down the passage, double speed.

I follow, Zeb close behind me.

"Again," he says, "it'd be a really good time to have a skateboard."

9

AFTER WHAT SEEMS like a thousand years, we arrive at the
bottom of the passageway, which is like an underground cave.

Henry and Zeb are inspecting the walls, which almost seem
a bit damp in the musty cold of the underground cavern.

"Whoa. Check this out." Zeb turns to us.

Henry and I inspect the wall where Zeb is looking. There
is writing.

"Is that Spanish? Kind of looks like Spanish." Zeb squints.

"It's Latin." Henry squints at the letters, carved like some old
graffiti in the side of the cavern. Pigeon scratches:

"fabulae non morietur

potest somnus solum legendas"

Zeb and I are both sounding it out, probably butchering it.

"Fab—u-lay. Non. Mori—eter. Po-test Some-nus. Sooo-lum. Legend-us."

Henry figures it out. Of course:

"Legends cannot die.

Legends can only sleep."

He turns to us. We both look back at him.

"Kind of sounds like something you'd hear them saying on, like, that E! channel or something. You know?" And Zeb is right.

"Well, maybe we're supposed to say it or something," I suggest. "Maybe it's an *incantation.* So if we say it, something will happen."

"You mean like a door will open so we can get out of here?" Zeb asks.

"Or, perhaps the ghosts we were promised will finally arrive," Henry suggests.

"That would be sick!" Zeb grins excitedly.

"Right," I say. "So perhaps we should all say it together. In tandem."

Zeb nods. "Okay, one, two, three!"

"Fabulae non morietur potest somnus solum legendas!"

We all say it in synchronicity, expectant and loud.

Then we listen, possibly waiting for a puff of smoke, a tremor in the earth, or perhaps a giant boulder rolling toward us.

Nothing.

No. Thing.

Just exactly as it was before.

Not even a shift in the air.

We look at one another, each of us feeling rather stupid.

"Well, that was anticlimactic," Henry admits.

"Maybe we should have had wands or something . . . ?" Zeb says.

I fold my arms. "This isn't Hogwarts."

Zeb shrugs. "You're the one who was talking about *family ghosts* or whatever."

The three of us stand there, at a loss for words.

Our sullen silence is interrupted, however, when we hear a distinct voice echoing down the chamber.

"You ever find those stupid kids?"

I'd know that voice anywhere.

The Midwestern Mastermind.

In pursuit.

Of us!

10

WHEREVER THE VOICE is coming from, it's not the direction we took. However, the Midwestern Mastermind's voice is definitely getting *closer*.

The three of us look around for somewhere to hide as the footsteps grow louder and louder.

"I really don't give a rat's—"

The static from his walkie-talkie drowns out the rest of his thought.

"But, boss, we have to go *now*."

"Listen here, you little yellow-bellied coward. There is no way I am leaving the premises, after all this planning, with nothing but a few random paintings! This is the heist of the century!" The Midwestern Mastermind stops, thinks. "And we better not leave any witnesses."

"Boss?"

"You heard me."

Henry, Zeb, and I share a look. No *witnesses*. You know what that means, don't you?

It means curtains. For everyone here.

We have to do something.

"I'm just stuck down some dank hallway. I thought you said there was some ancient stuff down here!" the Midwestern Mastermind barks.

More static.

"You better get up here, boss. The natives are getting restless."

"Yeah, all right, I'm coming. But you know what to do if anyone tries to be a hero," the Mastermind replies.

He turns, and we can hear his footsteps retreating back up the hallway to wherever he came from. The static follows him like the inside of what must be his brain, at this point.

Scrrrkkk. Scrrrrk Scrrrk.

The footsteps go silent as the three of us assess this new situation.

"Is this really happening right now?" Zeb asks. "Do we have to save the entire wedding from certain doom?"

"I'm afraid it most assuredly is," Henry answers.

"Rad," Zeb breathes. "And just so you know, after today, I plan on hanging out with both of you *way* more often."

11

BY THE TIME we emerge onto one of the thousand landings of this labyrinth, the rain is already creating miniature lakes all over the outside stones. I guess irrigation wasn't quite up to today's standards back when the castle was built.

There's a staircase leading up to what appears to be a lengthy corridor, door after door after door. From the ornate look of the doors, this is definitely not maids' quarters. Heavy mahogany with black ironwork underneath stone arches. Doors made to impress.

The three of us duck into the first one, finding ourselves in what must be the most exquisite of all the rooms thus far. A giant four-poster bed with a canopy lords over the room of burgundy velvets and damask. Oil paintings from the Renaissance look down at us, the figures' muscles visible beneath their skin.

"This must be some sort of guest quarters," Henry assesses.

"Some guest," Zeb quips.

As if in response, we hear the sound of splashing water coming from the smaller attached tiled room, the door slightly ajar. A bathroom. And now the sound of someone clearing their throat. A man.

As the three of us inch closer and closer, not wanting to see what we are hearing or hear what we are seeing, the sound of the splashing, and even a little hum, a meaningless, trifling little hum, come wafting out over the horizontal tile.

From where we are standing now, on the other side of a cherrywood vanity with a needlepoint stool, we can see the ivory shape of the end of a claw-foot tub, the claws of the tub in gold. Of course.

And, as we shuffle forward, we can see more of the white tub.

And, as we shuffle forward, we can see a toe coming out of the tub. Not a woman's toe. Or, if it's a woman, it's a woman with extremely hairy toes.

Now a foot.

We lean forward, now almost drawn by a magnetic field.

The water, foamy, filled with bubble bath.

And now a newspaper.

A newspaper?

And just as we lean forward a smidge more, one of us (which we will all blame on one another later, by the way) accidentally topples a mother-of-pearl hairbrush over onto the floor.

Crash!

The sound of the hairbrush is not subtle on the parquet floors, echoing through the enormous stone chamber.

"Good heavens!"

And the newspaper comes down, down to the level of the bathwater, and there, staring at us with a rather judgmental look usually reserved for magistrates or nuns, is . . .

Winston Churchill.

12

NOW, YOU MAY ask, *Who on Earth is Winston Churchill*? I'm not here to question the quality of your education, so I'll just tell you. Let's just get it all out on the table, shall we?

About seventy years ago there was this little, well, not so little, actually, world war, called World War II. Yes, there was a World War I, as well, but just to make sure they figured out that war was terrible, they had another one. The whole world. At war.

Now, this war was particularly diabolical for a myriad of unspeakable reasons that really should be explained by a nur-turing, kind, gentle, *not totally stressed-out* person whose life is not in peril and is definitely not me.

However, as in all things terrible, there is always a glimmer of hope, a light in the darkness, and for this particular war, that light in the darkness was he who sits bathing before us—none other than Winston Churchill.

There are as many scholars as there are rooms in this ginormous estate who would say that the war, *World War II*, was won because of *this man*.

So, he's like a thing.

A big thing.

But alas, this particular big thing *died over fifty years ago*.

And yet, right about now, he is before us in all his bathtubby glory.

"Henry, are you seeing what I'm seeing?" I muster.

"Yes, Eva. Most definitely."

"Wait, what are you guys seeing?" That's Zeb.

Of course. He can't see him. That would be way too easy.

We, Henry and I, are the ghost summoners, the ghost whisperers, the ghost . . . catnip, for lack of a better word.

Lucky, lucky us.

As I look closer I realize that good old Winston is surrounded by a kind of gray-blue shimmering. Yep. Not cosplay. Definitely a ghost.

"Do you plan on sitting there gawking, children, or is there a purpose for this rather inopportune visit?"

His voice a tenor grumble.

"We just, um, we just were—" I can barely contain myself.

"Well! Out with it! We were just what, dear child?!"

Henry composes himself.

"Sir Winston. Prime Minister of Britain. Your lordship—"

"I don't intend to sit here all day listening to my many titles uttered from the mouths of babes. Come now, boy!"

"We were hoping to—"

"Do you know you're a ghost?" I sputter out.

There's a silence now.

Winston Churchill looks at us with indignity. Zeb is, also, looking at us like we've caught the last ticket to crazytown.

You could hear a mouse burp.

"BAH-HAH-HAH!"

The sound erupts from the bathtub, splashing the water all around in bubbles and suds, drowning the tile hexagons.

"Why, my dear children, of course I *know*. What do you think I'm doing here?"

"I'm sorry. Why are you—" Henry leans in.

"You're the ones who summoned me!"

Summoned? My mind flashes back to the incantation in the basement, down the swirly-whirly ramp.

"The incantation." Henry stares up at me with we-are-the-luckiest-people-in-the-world shining in his eyes. "*Fabulae non morietur potest somnus solum legendas*. Legends cannot die. Legends can only sleep . . . ?"

He turns to Winston Churchill, who is waiting patiently in the tub.

"We need your assistance. It's quite desperate."

At this I feel the need to cut in. Henry is just too polite at times.

It comes out in one sentence. "The thing is we are trapped up here, in Hearst Castle, just to be sure we're on the same page as to where we are, we were supposed to be at a wedding, but then this roughed-up stranger interrupted the ceremony and practically all the guys and some of the ladies went down to save the town, well, it's not really a town, more of a hamlet really, not the play *Hamlet*, like an actual itty-bitty town sometimes called a hamlet, and then it turns out *that* was all a ploy to get all the cops and security and able-bodied folks, actually, down the hill so the real bad guys could steal all the art and jewels and statues and maybe rugs *in here*, although the rugs seem to still be up for debate, and they've taken everyone hostage and they said everyone should just stay still and everything will be fine but now we overheard them, the Midwestern Mastermind that is, and he says they're supposed to *leave no witnesses!*"

Silence.

I take a breath.

That was a long sentence. No question. My second-grade English teacher would not be proud.

"We see ghosts. My brother and I. Mostly, the ghosts of our ancestors. And well, they're the ones who told us to go to the basement and say the incantation. They said *you* could help with the . . . the Mastermind."

Winston peers at me over his glasses.

He regards me for what seems like three hundred years.

"I see." He frowns. "And who came up with the name 'Midwestern Mastermind'?"

"I did . . . sir," I defer.

"Quite so. Very pithy."

And now a glow seems to emanate from him and there is a twinkle in his eye. As if, perhaps, there is something in him that loves a good fight.

"Well then," he says, "to best a mastermind, we're going to need a few friends."

13

IF YOU'RE WONDERING what Zeb's been doing this whole time it's mostly sitting crisscross-applesauce on the chaise lounge and meditating. Of course, he can't see the esteemed Winston Churchill over there in the bathtub. He can only see Henry and me, talking to a bathtub.

To his credit, I'm sure most people would say, "Hey, that's great you are talking to a bathroom utility, but I have some homework I just randomly remembered so I better hit the road." But not Zeb.

From the other side of the room, we hear the sound of his chanting.

"Ohhhhmmm."

Winston looks past us toward Zeb on the chaise.

"Good heavens, that boy's hair is blue! Was he dipped in an inkwell?!"

"No, Mr. Churchill, that's our friend, Zeb. He's from Los Angeles."

"I see . . . And what is he doing, exactly?"

"Winston, Mr. Churchill, I really think we should get back to the matter at hand. Aka, the horrible heist and the *leave-no-witnesses* element." I try to veer him back, although he keeps furrowing his brow at Zeb.

"Ohhhhmmm."

"Did Gandhi put him up to this?"

"Gandhi! Certainly not, sir," Henry chimes in. "It's just . . . this is what everyone does now, to alleviate stress."

"Everyone?"

"Well, everyone in California," I add. "But please, Mr. Churchill. We need your help—"

"No, no, dear children. You do not need a chubby old man lumbering around on your behalf. What you need is *strategy*. Strategy and faith. And the others. Just remember . . . If you're going through hell, keep going."

And now the suds start to disappear into the ivory of the bathtub, Winston's glasses and cigar start to fade, even the newspaper turns to nothing more than a chiffon wisp.

I don't want him to leave. I have so many questions!

"Wait, no! But you haven't helped—"

"It was a pleasure meeting you, Prime Minister." Henry does a kind of awkward bow.

"Indeed, dear boy." And just as he is about to fade back into our imagination . . . a last bit of wisdom from beyond.

"Children, they shall expect you to be weak. They shall expect you to quit." He nods. "That is why you must . . . never, never, never give up."

And in a blink, he is gone.

14

I FIND MYSELF wishing Zeb could also see the ghosts. Because if he had seen Winston Churchill, *the* Winston Churchill, well, I'll be honest with you . . . I think he would have been inspired.

I know I was.

And so was Henry.

The two of us stand in awe, still basking in the luminescence left far after Winston's ghost has disappeared. A brush with greatness!

And then there are his words: *Never, never, never give up.* I mean, this is a man who thwarted the worst baddies of all time through sheer will and strategy. Yes, the Allied forces did the fighting, but would they have been so nimble, so inspired, without him? It was the frame he put around it. The story he told. He told a story about the good guys having to win. About grit, hope, and faith. I resolve to tell myself that story. Whenever I face something impossible: grit, hope, and faith. I will never, never, never give up.

Like now, for instance. In this situation, I could easily fall into despair. Into doubt. After all, Winston left us with nothing but a few pretty words. I could tell myself we are up the creek without a paddle and there is nothing to be done. But I can't tell myself that story. Because if I tell myself that story, Henry will start to tell himself that story, too. And then Zeb. And the three of us are the only bulwark against this dastardly crew.

"Strategy." Henry interrupts my train of thought. "Winston said we cannot defeat them with brawn. Only brains. We must think of a strategy."

"All for one and one for all?" Zeb chimes in.

"That's more of a slogan," Henry contemplates.

"Live long and prosper," Zeb offers.

"Okay, that's Star Trek," I add.

"May the Force be with you," Zeb throws out.

"Annnnnd that's Star *Wars*." I smile.

"No, no, no. These are all just slogans! We need an actual strategy."

"Oh, I know, I know. When the going gets tough, the tough get going!" Zeb suggests.

"Again, a slogan."

"A bird in the hand beats two in the bush!"

"Slogan."

"Divide and conquer!" Zeb offers.

"Wait . . . what was that?" Henry asks.

"Divide and conquer." Zeb stops for a moment. The air is still.

"That's it!" Henry turns to me. "Eva, didn't you say there was some *issue* . . . some *thing* the Midwestern Mastermind kept going on about?"

"Well, he was pretty much mad about everything but . . . I guess he kept getting super annoyed about . . . the rugs?" I recount.

"What, exactly, about the rugs?" Henry asks.

"He didn't want them to take the rugs because they were too cumbersome, and the guys wanted to. They said they were worth a lot," I answer.

"Okay! Now we're in business! We need to get ahold of one of those walkie-talkies." Henry is excited now, pacing about the room, wheels turning in his head.

"We do?" Zeb asks.

"Yes, most definitely." Henry paces more. "It sounds to me like the Midwestern Mastermind has hired this crew and doesn't exactly respect them. Perhaps he's exploiting them. That is something we can take advantage of. . . ." He's churning, feet going back and forth across the floor. I'm not sure I follow his train of thought quite yet.

"Okay, so, um . . . how do you think we should go about getting one of those walkie-talkies?" I ask.

"Distraction."

"And, um, who is going to be doing the distracting?" I ask.

"Eeeny, meeeny, miney, mo, catch a tiger by his toe . . ." Henry is already deciding. "If he hollers, let him go, my mother says to pick the very best one and you are not it."

His finger is pointing at me. We both turn to Zeb.

"Well, Zeb, looks like you're it. Can you think of a distraction?"

Zeb contemplates. "Yes. No. Maybe."

Henry and I smile.

"Maybe it is! And remember," Henry claps him on the shoulder, "divide and conquer!"

15

THE CATS AND dogs raining out of the sky are not letting up. They have become cougars and wolves. Buckets and buckets from the sky. It's like the clouds have been hoarding for months, months, and more months, and now it is all coming down in one fell swoop. One night carrying all the rain for the whole year.

The only lights on in the castle seem to be emanating from the great hall, where the wedding guests are still gathered. I still can't believe they're all just sitting there. But then again, those guys don't exactly look like happy little friendly Smurfs. Honestly, they look more like Smurf-crushers.

Never give up, Eva. Remember.

On the west-facing terrace, looking out to sea and the road

down to the PCH, now closed, there is a guard walking back and forth. He's not menacing, exactly. More like a guy just doing his job. Punching the clock.

Henry and I hide behind a giant bougainvillea-covered trellis while Zeb creeps up the back of the terrace. Neither of us really know what he has planned, but you would assume it involves a lot of sneaking.

Which is why it makes absolutely no sense when Zeb just walks up to the guy.

There is the guard, sinister, walking back and forth, and then, two seconds later, there is Zeb. Just standing right there in front of him.

"Hey, dude. I just wanted to see if I could get you anything . . . Water? Coffee? Maybe a Red Bull? I know, uh, heists can be exhausting sometimes and, you know, maybe they take longer than maybe you were expecting them to—"

"Tsh. Tell me about it," the guard says. "To tell you the truth, this guy who hired us, he's kind of a jerk." The guard shakes his head. "You know, maybe I will get a water."

"What?"

"You asked if I needed anything. Maybe I'll get like a water. Like a bottled water? One that's alkaline balanced, if you have it. You know, like the right pH level? You can't just drink any water. It has to have the right pH level or your body will just stay thirsty," the guard informs Zeb.

Henry and I look at each other.

"You're from California, aren't you?" Zeb asks.

"Dude, totally. You are, too. Right, little bro? I can tell."
The guard seems to have taken a shine to Zeb. I feel like everyone takes a shine to Zeb. He just sort of . . . glows or something.

"Yeah, I'm from LA. Los Feliz. Born and bred."

"See, I knew it!" The guard smiles. "I'm from Redondo."

I look at Henry. He shakes his head. This guy must be the dumbest criminal of all time.

Zeb nods. A walkie-talkie is on the bench, next to the guard. Guess he didn't feel like carrying it.

"So, uh, you know, I've always wanted to get into the, uh, thievery game. How does one go about it?" Zeb inquires.

The guard imitates him. "How does one go about it? Ha! You're a trippy little dude. Wull, I guess one goes about it by just . . . not having much going on, pretty much."

"Yeah, I bet your boss is raking it in though, right? I mean, I can't believe he's only paying you guys . . ." Zeb thinks. He's plotting, somehow. "Ten grand."

"Ten grand?!" The guard turns on a dime. "Who's getting ten grand?! I'm not getting ten grand. I'm only getting five grand. Who the heck is getting ten grand?!"

Zeb senses the vulnerability. Now he lays it on strong.

"Oh, like those guys who were talking inside, the guards for the wedding people. I heard them say they're both getting like ten grand each."

"That is so messed up! Those are the guys who roped me into this! They told me we were all getting the same. Five grand!"

"That is so uncool, dude. They totally snaked you. You

should just like bail. I mean, I heard that guy, your boss or whatever. He sounds really abusive," Zeb commiserates.

Henry and I are leaning in. Wow, Zeb is a mental ninja! Sowing confusion. Dissent. Resentment.

Dividing. But will we conquer?

"Tell me about it, bro. He's like always yelling, like the whole time. Like just a jerk." The guard is so annoyed.

"Is he from California, too?"

"Totally not. That's like his problem. He's like a ball of stress. I mean, he really needs to meditate or something. Take some yoga." The guard shakes his head. "Ten grand?! Man. That's just wrong. Whatever happened to equal pay for equal work, you know?"

Zeb comes in. "I know, dude."

"We're idiots." He looks at the ground. "I didn't even know the mark, honestly. If I'd known we were hitting *Hearst Castle* I woulda been like 'I'm out.' I mean, who the heck takes on Hearst Castle?!"

"Right? I mean, you guys could really get busted. And if you do, that could mean like . . . *life. In jail.*" Zeb coaxes.

The guard is now shaking his head. Wow. I actually feel sorry for him. What is happening here?

"Why did I ever agree to do this for five grand?"

Zeb shakes his head. "Have to make a living, I guess."

"Oh, dude, you don't know! I'm trying to like move out. My roommate's a total loser. Like he just walks around in his underwear all day and never does the dishes. And. And . . . all he ever watches is *Forensic Files*. Like day and night. Just one case after another!"

"Aw man," Zeb commiserates.

"And like, the other day, I was in bed and I felt something . . . and it was an ant. There's like ants everywhere. He's always eating sandwiches and leaving them, like, half-eaten everywhere. Just like, on top of the TV. What's that? Oh, it's a half-eaten peanut butter and jelly sandwich. Covered with ants!"

Zeb shakes his head. "So, the five grand is to pay for the move out?"

"Yep."

"Well, dude, I gotta tell ya. I don't think it's worth it. This guy is gonna get so busted. Then you'll be moving out all right. But you'll moving into . . . jail."

Henry and I share a look. I really can't believe this is happening.

The guard is just looking forward, shaking his head. "I know. It's like I'm watching a car crash. In slow motion."

Zeb leans in, and I really do get the impression that he actually does care, at this point. "Dude, it's not too late."

"What do you mean?"

"It's not too late. Your friends lied to you. You didn't know what you were getting into. You're barely getting paid anything. You could just . . . bail."

"Not really. I'm in too deep."

"It's never too late to change your situation. That's what my dad's life coach says. If you don't like your circumstances . . .

just change them. Don't think about it. Just do it."

"I dunno. . . ."

"Give yourself a second chance, dude. You could like, I don't know, open your own gym or be a dog whisperer or like trick out cars or something."

"I am really good with dogs." He straightens with pride. "I have a way with animals."

"See, that's what I mean!"

The guard deliberates.

SCRRTTCCHH. SCRRTTCCHH.

The walkie-talkie crashes this fine moment with gusto. But that's not the worst of it.

Zeb and the Redondo Guard look at the walkie-talkie. The horrible words come out, in the voice of the Midwestern Mastermind.

"Did you find those kids yet?! You can't miss them, I hear one of them has blue streaks in his hair, for criminy!"

Zeb and the Redondo Guard look at each other.

BUST. ED.

Zeb chuckles. And smiles wide. "My point still, uh, stands?"

There's about five thousand years of silence going on here, while Zeb and the Redondo Guard assess this new situation.

Then . . .

The Redondo Guard speaks, dead serious: "Looks like you have a date with the boss."

Zeb's face sinks.

Henry's eyes go wide with panic.

And then . . .

"*Ha!* Little dude! You should see your face! Oh my God, I totally got you!" The Redondo Guard laughs.

We all stare in shock.

The Redondo Guard imitates himself. "*Looks like you have a date with the boss.* Who talks like that?" He slaps his own knee and laughs.

Zeb's face goes from minor key to major, the light coming back into it.

"Oh my God. I've never been more bummed to have blue streaks," he confesses.

"I know, right?" The Redondo guard is still chuckling to himself. "C'mon, little bro, do you really think I'm gonna turn some little kid in to *that* evil dude? No way. I am not that guy!"

The two of them sit there in a moment of relief, a kind of collective exhalation.

Then, the guard takes a deep breath.

"All right. The heck with it."

And, before I know it, he takes the walkie-talkie and wipes it off for prints. Places it down on the bench and looks at Zeb.

"I'm out."

Zeb looks at him. "Really?"

"Yeah, that seals it. Sayonara, suckers!"

Zeb calls after him. "Dude, but can you help us with—!"

But the guard is already skittering down the hill, through the brush. He looks left and right, making sure no one sees him. Then he goes farther, sneaking from bush to bush, making his way down the path and back to a life of freedom. Roommate to an annoying half-sandwich leaver, but one with his liberty!

Zeb looks after the guard with a bit of pride as he makes his way farther and farther in the rain. Down the hill and, hopefully, back to his ant-infested apartment.

Now Zeb looks back at Henry and me, who stare at him in astonishment as he grabs the walkie-talkie.

Henry looks up at Zeb in wonder.

"You should be a . . . a lawyer."

"A *magic* lawyer," I agree. "Now let's fire up that walkie and see what chaos we can sow!"

16

"I LITERALLY CANNOT believe that just happened." Henry's still looking at Zeb like he's a Martian. "It was truly astonishing. It goes totally against the tenets of Maslow's hierarchy of needs. Could the need for human connection have overwhelmed the necessity for money?"

"Well, the guy didn't really *need* the money. What he needs is to have a conversation with his roommate. He seemed like a good guy. Just made a stupid decision. I hope he *does* become a dog whisperer. The world needs less greed, and more whispering."

"How did you know?" I ask.

"How did I know what?"

"How did you know about the measly payment?"

Zeb shrugs. "I just figured this guy, the Midwestern Mastermind, was a jerk, so probably a cheapskate to boot."

I shake my head. "I can't believe he convinced them to commit a horrible crime like this for five thousand dollars."

Zeb frowns. "Some people on the chessboard are just pawns. Just pawns to be moved around, used, and counted out by the honchos and bosses, the kings and the queens. It's not fair. It's just not a fair world."

Wow. That's . . . pretty deep.

I stare at Zeb, and for the millionth time I can see why Henry likes him. And I realize in that same moment that for some reason, I'm angry. And I can't figure out *why* I'm angry.

The three of us share a moment of silence.

Henry looks at Zeb. "You possibly saved that man from a miserable life in prison! With only your words. Well done, Zeb."

And this very pithy remark, too, somehow irks me.

What is wrong with me?

"Speaking of the police, why aren't they here yet?" Zeb asks.

"It's the inclement weather. And the lack of cell phone service. They have no idea what's happening. Otherwise, they would logically be here already." Henry thinks.

I gasp. "What if there was a trap? Set to ensnare both the police and the do-gooders from this very mansion?"

"A trap? You mean, down in the town?" Zeb ponders.

"Yes," Henry picks up the thread. "Some sort of fail-safe to make sure neither the authorities nor the vigilante mob would return. Perhaps they're in a basement somewhere in town, tied up and guarded just like these wedding guests here."

"Right." I think. "The bad guys' strategy was *also* divide and conquer."

"Precisely." Henry nods.

"You guys are like, whoa. Mega brains." Zeb smiles.

There's a statue below us, centered on the landing, of three ladies flimsily dressed. They might be goddesses but whoever they are, they look cold. I notice something luminous behind them.

"Guys." Henry and Zeb turn to me.

I point to the glowing thing. "Look!"

There down below, a shining figure puts three shining fur coats on the exact statues I was looking at.

"I don't see anything." Zeb squints into the rain.

"Wait. Is that . . ." Henry strains to see.

"Another ghost," I finish.

"But who?" Henry asks.

He's wearing a beige top hat, and a mop of blond curly hair sticks out underneath the brim. His matching trench coat billows around him.

"I'm not sure. I—"

Then another figure joins him. Heavy eyebrows. Glasses with eyes that roll wildly behind the lenses. Tuxedo. A half-burnt cigar between his fingers.

"You know, ladies," he addresses the statues, "I've had a perfectly wonderful evening, but this wasn't it!"

Henry gasps. "That's Groucho Marx! And his brother—what was his name again?"

"Harpo!" I cry. Dad used to love watching old Marx Brothers movies. Black and white. Totally weird. Their jokes were always about wordplay. They would say stuff like, "I could dance with you till the cows come home . . . but I would rather dance with the cows till you come home." Hilarious. Dad would roll on the floor, even though he knew all the jokes by heart.

"One of the Marx brothers?" Zeb asks. "Are you seeing a ghost of one of the Marx brothers? This is *so* coool!"

"It's *two*, actually." I roll my eyes at Zeb.

That mop of blond hair in a top hat winks at us and then disappears behind the statues.

Groucho, on the other hand, comes walking up the steps toward us.

"Eva, are you seeing this?" Henry asks.

"Groucho? Oh, yeah. I'm seeing it."

"Dying. I'm dying of envy right now," Zeb adds. "I'm like peanut butter and jealous."

Groucho reaches us on the landing.

"All right, kids, if you're looking for wisdom, here goes . . ."
Henry and I lean in.

"A black cat crossing your path signifies . . . that the animal is going somewhere." He puts his cigar in his mouth and raises his eyebrows.

Henry and I look at each other.

"No?" He continues. "How 'bout this: One morning I shot an elephant in my pajamas. How he got in my pajamas, I'll never know."

Henry and I can't help but smile.

"There. That's more like it." He grins. "Don't mind my brother over there." He gestures toward the three statues, now covered in glowing fur coats. "He can't get enough of that fur coat gag."

"Mr. . . . Marx? An honor to meet you," I say.

"An honor to meet me, too," he replies. "Now if you don't mind, I have to meet Mae West in the game room. She cheats at checkers, by the way."

Groucho flicks his cigar and begins walking up the steps. Henry and I stare dumbfounded behind him.

"Oh, one last thing, kids. Remember: *imitation is the greatest form of flattery.*" He tips his glasses. He smiles, fading up the stairs and into the night sky.

"But—stop!" I yell. "Wait! We need your . . ." It's too late. Groucho and Harpo are both gone.

Zeb interrupts our moment of awe. "What'd he say?"

Henry turns to Zeb. "Imitation is the greatest form of flattery. Among other things."

"Imitation . . . huh?" Zeb frowns.

The three of us stand there, pondering.

SKRRREECCCH!

Walkie-talkie static ends our contemplation.

SKRRREECCCH. SKRRREECCCH!

The three of us look down at it. Frozen.

"What is taking you dillweeds so long? We've got half an hour to hightail it out of here!" Unmistakably, the Midwestern Mastermind.

The three of us look at one another, listening.

"Look, boss, it's taking a little longer to load the statues. They're really, *really* heavy." The voice on the other side sounds more casual.

"Really? The *marble statues* are heavy? How 'bout that? I can't believe it! *Front page news!*" The Midwestern Mastermind's voice sounds like it comes right out of his nose.

"You don't have to be mean about it . . ." Casual Guard replies.

"And find. Those. Kids! God, I hate children." He mutters before he clicks off.

"Gah, that guy is the worst—" We hear Casual Guard say to his friend before there is a tiny *blip* sound, and the connection goes dead.

"Imitation! Mastermind said he was keeping his walkie off unless he wanted to talk to his henchmen." Zeb picks up the walkie-talkie.

"No, Zeb, what are you doing!" I reach out.

But it's too late.

Before we know it, he pushes the button.

SKRRREECCCH.

"Yeah, boss?" The casual guard tries not to sound annoyed.

Zeb puts the walkie-talkie to his mouth. And then it is Zeb talking, but it's not Zeb's voice. It's the voice of the Midwestern Mastermind. To a T.

Imitation.

"And don't forget the rugs!" Zeb commands, in the voice of the Midwestern Mastermind.

"But, boss, I thought you said that—"

Zeb continues in his fake nasal voice. "Lookit. I thought it out. You guys get the rugs. You can *have them*. See, you just got a raise, so you can stop complaining. Don't say I never did nothin' for you." Zeb winks at Henry and me, who both stand rapt before him and his Midwestern Mastermind accent.

He hangs up.

"See? Imitation."

Henry and I stare at him.

"Where did you learn to do that?" I ask.

"Do what?" Zeb replies.

"Do that . . . accent . . . perfectly?"

"Oh, yeah, my mom got this weird idea to make me famous or something and she put me in an acting class in the valley. I only went for like six months, but we did do accents. Then I quit. Because who wants to be famous? Like everywhere you go people just look at you like you're a Martian or ask you for an autograph or take a selfie while you're eating lunch and sell it and it's horrible and embarrassing. Ugh. What a life."

Henry and I stare at Zeb.

"How do you know though? About being famous?"

"My friend from kindergarten got super famous. He was in a bunch of movies and now he can't go anywhere. It sucks. Trust me," Zeb adds. "But the accents are cool, right?"

We nod. Zeb's Midwestern imitation is flawless.

"I'm impressed by this seed you've planted." Henry gives Zeb some props. "This rug issue may be just what the doctor ordered."

"Why, thank you, good chap." Zeb now sounds like he's from the high street in jolly old England. He pretends to tip his imaginary cap.

But I can't stop thinking about what he just said about being famous. All your life, everywhere you look, it seems like everyone is killing themselves to be famous. To be *someone*. But I never really thought about what that would look like, there on the ground. I never thought about how it would actually manifest itself on a daily basis. Is it really like that? Does it really feel like being trapped?

If that's true, then it's kind of a relief. I feel like it's something I can just cross off my to-do list. A reminder: DON'T BE FAMOUS.

SKRRREECCCH. SKRRREECCCH.

The walkie-talkie goes off.

"We should be out of here in half an hour, people! Did you get those kids yet? I want those kids!"

The three of us look at one another.

"*No* witnesses! Did you hear me?! *No* witnesses!"

17

WE MAKE OUR way back toward the chapel and grand hall.

The last thing I want is to have some sort of open confrontation with the Midwestern Mastermind, but it seems like these guys working for him are . . . malleable. Maybe even kind at heart.

But the Midwestern Mastermind is poised to make off with millions in stolen art, and I have no doubt in my mind he will do so *at any cost*.

I could see it in his cool stare when I was hiding behind the curtain. There's nothing behind his eyes. Not a soul. Not a conscience. Just someone who is used to a life of betrayal and backstabbing and every man for himself.

I wonder how a person even gets like that. Why is it that

some people veer so crazily off the tracks? Is it in their brains? Baked into the cake? Or is it something that comes from a life of disappointment after disappointment?

Why do some people become the Midwestern Mastermind and other people become Winston Churchill? Is it a plan? Or is it a process? I wonder . . .

"We have half an hour to save everyone in that room," Henry breaks in, nodding toward the wedding guests, still sitting, some lying down, as the guards watch over them.

"The rugs will slow them down," Zeb points out.

"But for how long?" I ask. "For. How. Long?"

The three of us ponder this.

"So, what do we do?" I ask. "I mean, divide and conquer is nice but pretty time-consuming. Maybe we should be more aggressive somehow. Considering."

Henry thinks.

But now there is a light down the hill, headlights splitting the rain into sheets. The three of us stare as a truck comes up the hill, hoping it's one of the parents returning to solve everything.

We watch the winding truck make its way up the serpentine little road, its wheels bearing into the mud. Clearly, whoever they are, they have super four-wheel drive.

The truck gets halfway up the hill when a light shines out onto it and one of the guards flags it down.

We three stare as an interaction takes place. It's impossible to hear what is being said through the pounding rain, but the

Hearst "guard" looks official, casual, nonplussed. He stands in an official way, gesturing back down the road.

The three of us watch as the interaction comes to an end. The truck driver nods, rolls up his window, and begins to execute a three-point turn, turning back down the road.

"The guard must have told him it's closed. Or it's a private party," Henry thinks out loud.

But there's no need to say anything. We three watch, deflated, as the truck rights itself and makes its way back down the hill, back down the coast, and to whatever little life awaits outside of this dire situation.

Almost.

We were almost saved.

And the three of us lose something watching that almost drive away, back down to wherever almosts go.

18

WE WILL HAVE to save the day.

With whatever means we have at our disposal.

Which, truthfully? Isn't a lot.

SKREEECCCCHH. SKREEECCCCHH.

The walkie-talkie interrupts this dirge, sending all three of us a foot in the air.

"Where are you idiots? I told you to meet me at loading dock!"

The Midwestern Mastermind is at it again.

"Yeah, we're coming, boss. We just have to load up the rest of the rugs."

Beat.

Henry, Zeb, and I freeze, waiting to see what will come next.

"The . . . what?" Midwestern Mastermind tries to control himself.

"The rugs."

"The rugs?! You mean the rugs I told you to absolutely, positively, *not* to worry about because they are cumbersome, you stupid imbecile!"

"Yeah, but, boss, you changed your mind and told us we could keep—"

"No. I did not tell you that."

"Did too."

"Did NOT."

"Did TOO."

"DID NOOOOOOOT!"

Silence.

"Did too."

"Oh sweet Jesus. What could possibly, in the ever-loving name of God be my reason for telling you such a dumb thing that I positively never told you!"

"Boss, you said we could keep the rugs, as part of the payment. We were . . . we were encouraged by your show of camaraderie."

"Camaraderie? There was no show of camaraderie. This is a job, get it? A job that *you* and your army of nincompoops keep screwing up!"

"I distinctly remember—"

"Do you know what this means?! This means we are off schedule! And do you know what happens if we get off schedule? . . . Well, do you?!"

"Not really."

"We get busted! Busted, you hear me?! We are on a strict time schedule and the further we're off the higher the chance that this whole thing, my whole ingenious plan that I've been plotting for years, goes down the tubes!"

"Wull. Maybe you should have left some wriggle room in the plan."

Mastermind loses it.

"Wriggle room?! What is this, romper room?! No, there is no wiggle room in the plan because the plan is perfect and the only thing that isn't perfect is you lot of popcorn heads!"

"That's mean."

"What?"

"It's just like so unnecessary to talk to us that way. It's like really just rude."

"Listen to me, you little whiny pinhead, if you don't get you and your whole crew down here in the next five minutes, I'll show you just how rude I can be! Got it?!"

He hangs up.

On the other line we hear the underling mutter, "It's just so disrespectful."

Then the line goes dead.

Henry thinks. "We should go down to the loading dock."

"But . . . the loading dock? That's where they're all going. Hello?!" I plead.

"Yeah, I mean, shouldn't we be going in the exact opposite direction?" Zeb asks. "They're all going there."

"Not anymore." Henry grabs the walkie-talkie, putting it to Zeb's mouth. Zeb smiles, getting it.

And now Zeb is imitating the Midwestern Mastermind again.

"Lookit, it's too late to meet down at the loading dock. Just stay where you are until I give the signal."

"Are you sure, boss?"

"Yeah, just stay put. Oh and . . . I'm sorry I was so abusive. It's just . . . this heist is really stressful."

"Okaaay. Thanks, boss. We just want to be taken seriously, you know?"

"Oh, I know. Okay, stay put until my signal. Over and out."

Zeb hangs up. Henry is staring at him like a groupie. And again, for some reason, my cheeks flame. I'm all hot. And cranky. What is happening?

"That was nice how you added in the respect part," Henry comments.

"You like that? I just felt kind of sorry for these guys, in a way."

"Perhaps they'll think the Midwestern Mastermind is schizophrenic," Henry ponders.

"Perhaps they will. But doesn't that help? Sow confusion and all?" Zeb adds.

"Oh, confusion is definitely being sown," I say. "I mean, *I'm* practically confused. Between the rugs, the ghosts, the loading docks, and the AWOL guard from Redondo I can safely say this has been quite a chaotic evening. I mean, this is the weirdest wedding I've ever been to."

And even though I know—like, I *know* this is a bad idea, I find myself following along, down the pathway around the castle, toward the loading dock.

19

THE LOADING DOCK is the only place in this joint that is not gold-gilded. It's mostly a study in gray, charcoal, white, putty color, and asphalt. Gone are the frescoes on the wall and the damask wallpaper. This is a place of sweat and low wages.

Henry, Zeb, and I are peering out from the alcove above, as below the many trucks back up, then forward, keeping their lights off, everyone trying to be as quiet as you can be when you are stealing millions of dollars' worth of statues, paintings, art, and general treasure. The three of us look around for signs of the Midwestern Mastermind, hoping to get a glimpse of him and suss out his escape plan.

So far though, it's only about three guys on the loading dock, five guys driving trucks, and lots of chaos.

And whispering. The whispering is us.

"Do you see him?" Zeb asks me. I am, after all, the only one who has seen our dearest villain in the flesh.

"No, not yet. Just look for the guy that is skinny as a stick, black hair, and really weird eyes," I say.

"Weird in what sense?" Henry asks.

"Weird in the sense that he kind of looks like he has purple makeup all around his eyes," I offer.

"You mean like he's tired?" Zeb asks.

"Sort of. But more like he's tired from . . . his whole life," I attempt. "Also, his eyes kind of look like he's in a constant state of surprise."

"You mean, as if he's realized that life is just a series of meaningless gestures leading slowly, inevitably into eternal nothingness?" The voice sounds familiar.

Henry and I share a look, turning to see none other than our ancestor ghosts. Maxine, Beaumont, Plum, August, and Sturdy. All just standing there next to us in the alcove, casual as can be.

"What . . . what are you guys doing here?" I ask.

"Um, who are you talking to?" Zeb still doesn't see them.

"Ancestor ghosts," Henry answers, as if it couldn't be more obvious. "They just appeared."

"Right, yeah. Totally." Zeb pretends this is normal.

"Welp, we just wanted to make sure you chickens were fightin' the good fight!" Beaumont exclaims.

"And that you weren't in any danger." Plum adds.

"And that you were socking it to 'em but good!" Beau cackles.

"And that you were being safe," Plum corrects.

"And that you were givin' them the old what what!" Beau does a fighting gesture.

"And that you were doing it with panache," August and Sturdy add.

"And that you were aware that, ultimately, none of this will matter, just as nothing, ultimately, does matter in this charade we call an existence, a life lived in spurts jumping around from one crisis to the next, not realizing that, in the end, it was all just a tale of walking shadows."

"Oh, don't listen to that sad sack! You kids got gumption! Grit, I tell ya!" Beaumont exclaims.

"And you are here for a reason," Plum chimes in.

"Heeeeere for a reeeeasoooon," August says in a spooky voice.

Sturdy gives him a look. "What's this?"

August retorts, "I thought I would embellish. To add . . . intrigue. Ghost it up a bit."

"Oh, quite right." Now Sturdy turns to us. "Heeeerrree for a reeeeassssooon."

"Oh, nicely done," August compliments him.

"Do you like it? I quite liked doing it," Sturdy responds.

"A reeeeeasssssonnnn," August adds.

"No, no. You have to have more of a singsongy voice. Like

this: Heeeerrrreee for a reeeeaaasoooon. Did you see? Sing-songy," Sturdy adds.

"Heeeere for a reasonnnn."

"A reeeeassson."

"It's like two dying hogs!" Beaumont interjects.

But Plum comes in over them. "It's true. You must know, dear children. You are here for a reason."

"ReeeeeeASSSONNN."

"REEEEEEEsoooon."

And as their singsongy voices fade out, so do their ghostly blue figures, leaving slowly the last of the singsongs and sapphire gloom. Until, at last, there is nothing.

Henry stares up to the spot where they disappeared.

"Eva, do you think it's possible that madness runs in our family?"

Zeb answers, "You mean madness like seeing random ghosts everywhere?"

"Exactly," Henry answers.

"Hmm." I think. "Well, perhaps. But if there is madness, there is method to it."

"Ah, Polonius. From *Hamlet*! 'Though this be madness, yet there is method in't.' Good one, Eva," Henry quotes.

"Why, thank you."

And I don't know why, but suddenly I'm happy. Happy in the midst of a heist! It doesn't make sense. I don't understand feelings!

"You guys!" Zeb interrupts. "Does that look like the guy? See, over there. Skinny. With dark hair. With weird purple eyes. And he's standing there with . . . with—"

He stops short. Henry and I look in horror as we see what Zeb sees.

"Binky?"

The three of us hold our breath as we stare agape at the Midwestern Mastermind leading Binky through the chaos below, her arms bound and a scarf tied around her mouth as a gag.

"Oh my God," I breathe. We look at one another.

"He's got the bride! Somebody do something!"

20

THIS IS JUST really adding insult to injury. Poor Binky. First, her wedding is interrupted by a demonic heist and now, second, she is being held hostage by a skinny, black-haired, nasal-voiced evil mastermind who has, remember, insisted on not leaving any witnesses.

I mean. How rude!

The least he could have done is pick someone else. There are plenty of other folks down in that wedding chapel just sitting there like a bunch of rump roasts. Why didn't he just pick one of them? Why did he have to pick the actual bride? The one and only Binky?

Okay, it's true, I wasn't a huge fan of Binky at first. Mostly, because I was being protective of Zeb's super-nice dad. I mean, his dad is like the dad of the century. Always making jokes and being goofy. My dad was like that. Like, whenever he saw a picture of that giant pointy white Washington Monument in Washington, DC, he would shake his head and say, "They'll never get it off the ground." Or, every time we were at a Chinese restaurant and Mom and Dad would open their fortune cookies, his would read, "Help! I'm trapped in a Chinese cookie factory!" You know. Dad jokes.

A lump forms in my throat. I swallow hard to banish it.

Sorry: Binky. I guess Henry has convinced me. Binky cares about her ridiculously elaborate wedding, so this taking-her-hostage thing is just beyond the pale. It's just not *done*.

I mean, it shouldn't need to be spelled out. Like—

Things not to do at a wedding:

1. Wear white.

2. Get crazy and dance into the chandelier.

3. Kidnap the bride.

"I can't believe this is happening," Zeb confesses.

"It appears the Midwestern Mastermind has decided to hold Binky hostage. Perhaps as a sort of insurance policy," Henry ponders.

"But what about not wanting any witnesses?" I ask. "She's more than a witness now."

The three of us think about this. Not wanting to think what it might mean for Binky.

"We have to do something." Zeb turns to us.

He's right, but what are we supposed to do? I mean, have any of *you* ever been in a situation where you have to thwart a castle heist and a bride-kidnapping operation.

I didn't think so.

"I've been in a lotta situations in my life. But I can't say none of 'em ever amounted to a pile of beans in the end."

Henry and I look at each other, then turn toward the voice, there on the other side of the alcove. There's a kind of smoky mist blowing through, revealing a man, svelte and handsome, a bit weathered, wearing a white tuxedo jacket, leaning against the railing, squinting at us through the smoke.

"Don't worry, kiddo. Things are never so bad they can't be made worse."

Another ghost. Our collective jaws drop to the ground.

At least, Henry's and mine do. It's not just another ghost. It's another *famous person* ghost.

Humphrey Bogart. The biggest star of his time. Like, if you took George Clooney and Brad Pitt and Tom Cruise *and* Tom Hanks *and* every single one of the Avengers and rolled them together and made movies with that guy.

That's how famous this ghost is.

Humphrey. Bogart.

How the heck will he help us?

21

NOW, IF YOU don't know who Humphrey Bogart is, don't worry. I won't blame you. It just so happens that our mother was obsessed with Humphrey Bogart and insisted, on long nights in the summer, on showing black-and-white film-noir movies featuring the one and only Bogie, as he was called. *The Maltese Falcon*, *High Sierra*, and, the most famous, *Casablanca*.

My regret, right this second, is that our mom cannot be here to see this. She would have catapulted four feet out of her shoes to be graced by the presence of this particular antihero.

"Looks like you kids got yourself in a pile of trouble." His forehead leans forward, an amused grin on his face. It's only now that I notice his little black bow tie.

"Yes, indeed, Mr. . . . Bogart," Henry mutters.

"Boggart?" Zeb can't see him, of course. "Like those things from Harry Potter?"

Henry pats his arm reassuringly. I smirk.

"No need to stand on ceremony, kid. It's just me." And, of course, he would see it like that.

"Mr. Bogart, sir, Humphrey. We don't exactly know what to do here." I explain, nervous. "We were at this wedding then, next thing you know, we're in the middle of a heist! Then, next thing you know, the Midwestern Mastermind—"

"Midwestern Mastermind? Who thought of that?"

"I did, sir," I reply.

"Cute, kid. Real cute."

"Then next thing you know the Midwestern Mastermind is saying *no witnesses*. Then, next thing you know he's kidnapped the bride. Then—"

"Then the next thing you know you've got yourself in a real pickle."

I stop.

"Exactly."

"Look, kid, the problem here is greed, pure and simple. Somewhere along the line one of these guys decided that money was the be-all and end-all of the thing. Only they don't know the truth. The only point in making money is, you can tell some big shot where to go."

"Right." I smile. "Right. But what do we do about it? Right now. I mean, how do we save the day?"

"Save the day? Look, kid, you wanna be a hero?"

Henry and I nod.

"All right, good. Then just remember, *not everything is exactly what it seems.*"

Henry and I nod, pretending we know what this means.

"But, um, when you say that do you—" But all of a sudden I am talking to no one. The smoke wisps over the railing right where he stood, in all his black-and-white glory. Now it's just an empty corner of the alcove, no longer graced with the presence of the world's wryest antihero.

Great. Just like the others. So very helpful.

22

"NOT EVERYTHING IS exactly what it seems," Henry repeats the words of wisdom.

Zeb looks at him. "Excuse me?"

"Not everything is exactly what it seems. That's what he told us, Humphrey Bogart," Henry explains.

"Oh! Right. Yeah, that's just like the time Elvis Presley told me, 'You lie down with dogs, you get up with fleas,' or when Abraham Lincoln advised, 'Don't judge a book by its cover,' or when Martin Luther King Jr. took me aside at my friend's bar mitzvah and told me never to count my chickens before they're hatched. . . ." Zeb jokes.

"Eva, what do you think it means?" Henry turns to me.

"I have no idea."

Zeb jumps in. "One time, Mohandas Gandhi said, 'Eat your broccoli.'"

That burning hot sensation is back in my face. There is a terrible feeling oozing through my veins that I still don't understand. I try to tamp it down as I seethe. "Gandhi is famous for using *hunger strikes* as a form of protest, so I very much doubt he said that at all!"

Henry and Zeb stare at me.

"Sorry, I just. Look, I'm a little bit concerned about Binky. Remember? The one who is over there being kidnapped? Your would-be stepmother?!"

We all look back at the loading dock. Binky is, indeed, being escorted, now by one of the lesser tweedle minions, to a black SUV near the back of the dock. I bet that must belong to the Midwestern Mastermind. Huh. I wouldn't have pegged him as a Cadillac type. But maybe that is exactly who he is.

Poor Binky. I can see the mascara smears from crying on the sides of her cheeks. That's the thing about wedding makeup. They really pile it on. It's like, "Hi, I'm your bride and I am also a cake face! Marry me!" I wonder who set the heavy makeup rule as the wedding norm. I mean, why doesn't the groom have to wear all that stuff? He's probably the one that needs it more.

"Okay, we have to think of a plan. Henry?" Zeb turns to him, expectantly.

"I take it you mean I have to think of a plan?" Henry quips.

"Well, yes," Zeb admits. "I mean, you're so awesome at it."

I fight the sudden lurch in my stomach. It feels like I'm going to hurl.

"All right, let's see . . ." Henry thinks.

SCCRRRTTTCHHH. SCCRRRTTTCHHH.

The walkie-talkie has a plan of its own. The three of us lean in, waiting to hear the next dispatch.

"Where the heck are you nitwits? We're behind schedule enough as it is!" The nasal tones of the Midwestern Mastermind puncture the airwaves.

"What?" The tweedle voice answers.

"I said, where the heck are you! I told you to meet me down here twenty minutes ago!"

"Down where?" Tweedle sounds confused.

"DOWN HERE! The loading dock, you meathead!"

"No, boss, you said to stay where we are and wait for your next order. I remember and so do the guys. . . . You guys remember that right? Right? . . . Yeah, the guys remember it, too. You told us to stay put."

"What are you talking about?! Have you lost your mind?! I told you to get the heck down to the loading dock RIGHT AWAY because we were already behind and now we are even MORE BEHIND, you dipstick!"

"You also said you would work on your abusiveness," the tweedle-guard replies.

"What?! What did you just say?"

"You actually apologized for being so disrespectful and said you would work on it—"

"I did no such thing! Why would I do such a thing! If I want to be disrespectful I am damn right going to be as disrespectful, mean, abusive, horrible as I want!"

"That's your choice, dude," Tweedle answers.

"Dude?! Did you just call me DUDE?! Now, listen to me. If you want this job, and you want the money, and you don't want to spend your whole life in prison, then you and your band of noodle-brains will get your butts over to the loading dock tout suite!"

"Tout what?"

"Tout. Sweet! It's French! Meaning RIGHT NOW!"

The Midwestern Mastermind hangs up. There's a *blip* as he switches off his walkie.

The three of us look at one another.

Zeb shrugs and picks up the walkie-talkie.

SCCCRTTTCCHH. SCCCRTTTCCHH.

"Hey, guys?" Zeb's Midwestern Mastermind voice is spot-on.

"Uh, yeah, boss?" Tweedle answers hesitantly.

"I'm really sorry about that."

"Um . . ." Tweedle doesn't know what to say.

"It's just, I need to work on my impulse control. It's a process. You know what I mean?" Zeb winks at us.

"Uh, yeah, boss, sure." I can hear the squiggle in tweedle-guard's squiggly mouth.

"Probably something to do with my blood sugar. Anyway, I've got it in under control here so you guys just meet me at the west gate," Zeb orders them as the Midwestern Mastermind.

"Uh, but you just said—"

"I know what I just said. But I changed my mind. The plan is more efficient this way. Think of it as a plan B. Go to the west gate. And I'll meet you guys there." Zeb is enjoying this.

"Uhhmmm. Okaaaay. We'll just be at the . . . west gate, then. Till you meet us," Tweedle answers.

"Nice. I really enjoy working with you guys. Teamwork. It makes the dream work." Zeb hangs up.

The three of us look at one another. Then we hear, over the walkie-talkie, the tweedle-guard talking to the other guards.

"Dude, this guy's a psychopath."

23

THERE ARE THINGS to be thankful for and there are things to be less thankful for.

Things to be thankful for:

1. Henry's brain.
2. Zeb's Midwestern accent.
3. Ghosts.

Things to be less thankful for:

1. This heist.
2. The Midwestern Mastermind.
3. Binky being kidnapped.
4. This strange grumbly feeling I get whenever Henry and Zeb are all *you're so awesome* with each other.

Basically, this is one of those moments in life where I feel extremely rich on the experience side but extremely poor on the relaxation side.

"I think the priority should be liberating Binky," Henry decides.

"I agree," I add.

"Totally." Zeb nods.

"Perhaps if one of us goes down there, creates some sort of distraction, while the other two slip behind the SUV and free her," Henry suggests.

"Well, maybe it should be Zeb. He can convince them all to give up like he did with that Redondo guard," I reply.

"Interesting. But I doubt it will work. Zeb struck a chord of one-on-one connection with our man from Redondo. One can hardly assume he will be able to fire up that same kind of camaraderie with a group," Henry assesses.

"That's true," I admit.

"Logically, it should be Eva. No one is looking for her. They don't even know she exists," Henry adds. "They're looking for two boys. One with blue hair."

Zeb and I nod. Yes, that's reasonable.

"Eva, can you think of something? Anything you can do to distract them?"

"Not really. I mean . . . maybe I could sing a song or something?" I offer.

Henry and Zeb are not convinced.

"What about a poem?"

"You can't be serious."

"I know, what about a musical number? The old song and dance. In costume. I bet I can really knock their socks off!" I suggest.

"Eva, they don't exactly strike me as Broadway folks," Zeb breaks it to me.

Grumbly feeling increasing. Though I have to admit he's right.

"Okay, well, let me just feel it out. I'm sure I can come up with something. . . ."

"Right. But there is a time issue here, so perhaps don't take quite so long to 'feel it out,'" Henry suggests.

"Like maybe just 'feel it out' super quick," Zeb adds.

And this is me, with zero ideas in my head, trying to "feel it out" on the fly . . . trying come up with something, anything, to distract a band of lethal, Broadway-averse ruffians.

24

THREE OF THE trucks have already departed the loading dock, and are sitting in a position behind the castle waiting for what I can only imagine is the all clear to take off. The other two trucks are still being loaded, the backs of the trucks open, looking like a grand bazaar of masterpieces waiting to be shipped off to faraway climes.

That leaves two trucks here. With two truck drivers. The guys I'm really worried about, though, are the two guarding the trucks and the one guarding the SUV. These guys are the great concern. They are heavily armed. Straps and holsters and rounds of ammunition hang off every possible part of their torsos (and some parts of their arms and legs).

Also, they're not exactly the hapless-looking tweedles we've run into thus far. *These* guys have a mean look about them—their mouths curled in what must be permanent snarls. Like, if they were dogs, instead of going in for an ear scratch or a belly rub, you'd absolutely cross the street to avoid them.

Henry and Zeb have run off to a passageway that spills out behind the truck, waiting for my signal.

I'm still figuring out the ins and outs of my epic distraction but so far all I have is a fake wound, the idea of hollering about a massacre inside the wedding chapel, and the hopes that all of this will add up to such a frightening sight that the guards will immediately run into the chapel and away from us.

I know, it's not perfect. But I am honing it as we speak. In the meantime, I have secured some ketchup packets from a discarded fast-food sack left abandoned in the loading dock. I will pour this ketchup all over myself in an effort to seem like I'm covered in blood and freak these guys out enough to believe my tale of woe.

There's a little window here, tucked into the gray stone, which is serving as a mirror, my reflection in the glass. It's perfect for practicing my act.

"Help! Help! You must come, it's chaos! Help, oh, no, the horror! My words cannot describe the terrors mine eyes have seen!"

Maybe that last one is going a bit too far. But you get the idea.

Using my teeth, I tear open the ketchup packets. I am about to squirt them into my hair (nothing is as terrifying, and bloody, as a head injury. I know. I am forever scarred by the time I knocked over Henry's rocket experiment and instead of launching into space it careened straight into his cranium.) when I see something strange in the little looking glass. There, off to the side. A sloping shadow in the corner of the reflection, probably just some illusion caused by the refraction of light in the rain.

Except that when I look closer I see it is not just a sliding shadow but an actual figure, an actual figure getting bigger and bigger in the reflection. Closer and closer. Coming toward me.

The hair on the back of my neck is standing at attention and I am frozen in panic as I realize what the almost imaginary figure is and where, exactly, it is heading to.

I turn around before it can reach me, willing myself to be strong, willing myself to never give up. I turn around even though every cell in my body is telling me to crouch down and skitter off like a scared little kitten and run deep into the downpour far, far down the hill and away from this place. I turn around and just in time, I see the walking shadow, the lurching figure reflected in the glass.

The Midwestern Mastermind.

25

DO YOU KNOW that moment? The moment on the roller coaster ride just before it's about to plunge into the abyss? Or, let's say, if you've ever been on one of the newer rides . . . when they tell you to cross your ankles and suddenly the ride starts and you're wondering why they were so insistent about your ankles?

But by then it's too late.

Well, that is this moment. Except there is no ride, no strapping in, and no insurance policies. There are no ride monitors, information desks, or theme park managers. No, sir. There is only little ol' me here, in the middle of the pouring rain, looking square in the face of a certain diabolical mastermind who has already made his intentions clear.

No witnesses.

Think fast, Eva!

This close to the Midwestern Mastermind, it's a little difficult to tell if he's annoyed, filled with hatred, surprised, or possibly just exhausted. I don't blame him. It's been a long day of heisting. If I were him, I'd just want to go home, sit back, Netflix, and binge. I would want to just take it easy.

That's it.

Make it easy.

He's looking at me like I am a problem to be solved. He's calculating. What do I do about this problem? Where do I put this problem?

Make it easy.

"Oh, hi. Um . . . bride or groom?"

"What?!"

"Bride or groom? Are you a guest of the bride or the groom?"

He looks at me, trying to stack up these Legos.

"Sorry, to be honest, I actually fell asleep in the reading room. Weddings are so boring and I just got back from white-water rafting with my dad, so I'm just like really tuckered out. How's the reception been going? Did they cheap out with a cash bar? I doubt it, knowing Binky, but people do that, you know? Fancy that . . . you make all the effort to go to a wedding and then you have to pay for your own soda?!"

I'm just repeating a conversation I heard at one of Terri's cocktail parties. I really have no idea what I'm talking about but I'm just trying to make the problem, i.e., the problem of me existing in this particular place and time, go away for ye ol' Mastermind.

"Kid . . ." He looks at me. "What's your name?"

"Daffodil!"

(I don't know why I shout it out like that. Or why I choose Daffodil. It just sort of blurts out.)

"Daffodil?"

He looks at me.

I nod.

"God, I hate California."

"Really? I have to say I think we have a lot of things to recommend ourselves. For instance, there's the weather. The foliage. Do you like bougainvillea? A lot of people really love bougainvillea. Fun fact: bougainvillea is actually a huge attraction for . . . wait for it . . . RATS! Can you believe it? I know I couldn't but—"

"Lookit, *Daffodil*." He strains through his stained crooked teeth. "This is a very . . . complicated catering operation. Everything has to be just perfect. You know how brides are." He winks.

Okay, so he's pretending, too. He's pretending to be the caterer.

(Let's just be honest, that's a stretch.)

But this is great. We're both pretending.

"Oh yeah, brides. I mean. Wow. I totally get it." I roll my eyes, pretending to commiserate.

"Right. Exactly. And that's why we can't really have any lit-tle kids back here, messing with perfection. So . . . what you're gonna do is, you're going to turn around and go back to the wedding chapel like a good little girl. Got it? *Daffodil?*"

"Oh, I got it."

He stays looking at me.

"Why am I still looking at you?"

"What?"

"Why am I still looking at your face? What did I. Just. Say?" He tries to keep a lid on it.

"Turn around and go back to the wedding chapel," I repeat back.

"Yes. Good." I'm definitely draining his last ounce of his patience here but I'm assuming he's going easy, trying to just pretend everything is normal, it's just catering, and get me out of here.

"Okay, cool, caterer guy. So, I'll just uh . . . get out of your way . . . and um . . . let you get back to creating the culinary magic, food magic, that is."

"That's right. Food magic." He nods, waiting for me to go.

I step back, first one step, then the next, then the next. Then the next. Until I make an oh-so-awkward "casual" turn around and do a brisk-walk-but-not-run-because-a-run-would-be-too-suspicious out to the end of the passageway.

Behind me, I can feel him boring a hole through my back with his eyes, making sure this problem is solved. This problem, i.e., me. The solution being that I am back with the others. Back with the other problems. All the problems left in the wedding chapel.

The witnesses.

I could take this time to contemplate the fate of everyone in the wedding chapel, or the fate of Binky, or the fate of all the people stuck down in the town below. I could take on all of their fates at this very moment and sink into the abyss trying to unwind this, trying to piece together this puzzle in a way that ends in a peaceful super-happy smiley way with nothing involving "no witnesses."

But that's not what is happening right now. Instead, as I turn the corner, out of the piercing gaze of the Mastermind, I collapse against the wall breathing so heavy, I feel like every statue in here is about to turn to me, put their finger to their marble mouth, and say, "Shhh."

Whatever is pouring down on me, it's not rain. It's sweat. Buckets of post-Mastermind perspiration, reminding me of how close I just came to almost getting hauled away to God knows where.

Maybe hauled away with Binky.

Oh God.

Henry and Zeb were on their way to rescue Binky.

And I was supposed to be the distraction.

Welp.

That was an epic fail.

26

LITTLE BY LITTLE, I start to take stock of where I have landed, winded, panting from the interaction with the Midwestern Mastermind. As if the leaves themselves are reaching out to me, reviving me, I begin to realize that I'm in a kind of garden, a mini garden near the back entrance to the chapel. A secret garden!

My mom had a secret garden, hidden between our house on the cliff and the cliff itself. You could walk past the edge of it a thousand times and not have any idea it was there. A row of hedges and willow acacia, behind it, a labyrinth of roses, hydrangea, and azaleas. There was a wooden bench in the middle and even a swing tied to a branch fifty feet above. That was my favorite thing to do, whiling away the afternoon, daydreaming on that swing.

But this secret garden is a more serious affair. The benches are stone and the different species of flower are ceremoniously marked with plaques: "Butterfly Mariposa Lily (*Calochortus venustus*)," "Douglas Iris (*Iris douglasiana*)," "Prickly Phlox (*Leptodactylon californicum*)." I'm beginning to realize that these are all native species of California when a funny thing begins to happen.

As I stand there, squinting at the lettering of the little bronze plaques, the flowers seem to be extending themselves somehow to me, growing toward me, and growing farther, growing longer, and then . . . sprouting new buds, and new stems, and new leaves, and flowers. As if the lifetime of each is sped up into seconds, a lifetime . . . and then another and another. The speed of the blooms is rapidly expanding, blossoming before me and all around me, forming a kind of archway, a floral and foliage archway, forging itself before my astonished eyes.

And then, there, in the middle of the archway, they appear. One by one.

"Dagnabbit! You were fast, fast I tell ya! Quick as lightning!" Beaumont slaps his knee, his eyes twinkling. "I said, that's my kin, all right. Right there! The apple doesn't fall far from the tree. One time I grifted my own way out of a grift! Way back in '33, why, these two fellas were fixin'—"

"Not now, Beaumont!" Plum interrupts. "Dear child, how frightened you must have been."

"Frightened?! Just look at her! She outsmarted that skinny

skunk in two seconds. Yessir, my kin. Right there. Wiley!"
Beau lights his corncob pipe.

"Huzzah, huzzah!" August and Sturdy raise their martini
glasses in a toast.

Maxine croons, "It was as best as it could be . . . as best as
anything can be in this foul and cruel world—"

"Oh, let's all just throw ourselves in the soup then!" Beaumont shakes his head.

"No need to throw ourselves in the soup, dears. Remember,
they're not out of the woods yet. . . ." Plum admonishes.

"Not even close! I don't even know which end is up! First,
the wedding gets hijacked. Then Winston Churchill appears in
a bathtub and then Humphrey Bogart shows up in the alcove
and tells us everything is not as it seems!"

"Nothing ever is . . ." Maxine mourns. "Nothing ever was.
And nothing ever will be—"

"Enough with the funeral march, let's get crackin'!" Beaumont puffs. "I bet he means someone's been duped!"

"Duped? What is duped?" August ponders.

"I think he means deceived, deluded, beguiled," Sturdy
replies.

"Hornswoggled! Bamboozled! Hoodwinked! Swindled!
Scammed!" Beaumont is now just yelling out words.

"Well, obviously. I mean. There's been a heist. There continues to be a heist. Even now. As we speak. In fact, we're kind
of just wasting time right now," I add.

"'There will be time, there will be time . . .'" Maxine

laments, "'To prepare a face to meet the faces that you meet; There will be time . . . Time for you and time for me, And time yet for a hundred indecisions, And for a hundred visions and revisions, Before the taking of a toast and tea . . .'"

"Doom and gloom! Doom and gloom!!" Beaumont snaps.

"My dear, there are deceptions." Plum comes forward. "And then there are deceptions within deceptions."

"Like double-deceptions!" Beaumont exclaims, excited.

"Unfortunate, unfortunate," August and Sturdy agree.

"You must listen to this Humphrey. These words carry wisdom. . . ." Plum nods, fading into the foliage behind her.

"Wait! Who is deceiving us? Why won't any of you be clear?"

The archway, the roses, the ivy all envelop the fading ghosts and I am left alone again in the middle of the secret garden.

A deception within a deception.

What on Earth could it mean?

PART THREE

1

THE RAIN HAS turned into a light drizzle now, causing me to wonder if this is a good thing or a bad thing, in terms of heist thwarting. If the roads let up, maybe there is a chance we will be saved. Or, on the other hand, maybe it means the Midwestern Mastermind and his tweedle army will be able to steal away, taking all the treasure and possibly our lives with them.

You see, positives and negatives.

Tiptoeing my way back through the brambles of the secret garden, I begin to hear a strange noise coming from the general vicinity of the loading dock. One by one, unmistakably now, I hear the sound of loaded engines roaring to life. The sound of each like a slumbering giant awakening to the drizzling night.

Then, one by one, I see the headlights of each truck, as if each one is a signal.

"Come on, we're leaving."

No. It can't be. They can't be heading out already! The heist can't be over. We can't have failed that quickly, or that finally. And what about the *witnesses*?

I look up to the light in the rows of arched stained glass windows of the chapel hall. The lights inside are flickering, no sign of a change within.

Chapel or loading dock?

Loading dock or chapel?

Maybe I should just stay here and do nothing.

Maybe the problem will take care of itself.

This is the last thought I have before I hear it.

2

"EVAAAAAAAAAA!!" THE SOUND of it echoes off the stone walls, and there, running toward me basically the fastest I've ever seen him running anywhere, is Henry.

"Henry! Here, I'm over here! What's happening? Where's Zeb?" I yell back.

Henry collapses in front of me, collecting his breath, his shoulders moving up and down, desperate.

"They have . . . They have . . ." He exhales. "They have Zeb."

He catches his breath, looking up at me, panicked.

"What? Who has Zeb?" I ask, holding Henry by the shoulders.

"The guards. They nabbed him when we tried to rescue

Binky." Now he looks at me. "Where were you, by the way?"

"I failed," I answer.

"I'll say."

"No, you don't understand. I ran into the Midwestern Mastermind—"

"You what?" Henry says with a start.

"I had to fool him. I had to think fast. I told him my name was Daffodil. I pretended I didn't know anything . . . look, it's a long story. What do we do about Zeb?"

"I'm not sure. We have to save him." He looks up at me.

"Wait. How did you get away?" I ask him.

"I ran, obviously. It's not exactly my forte." He looks at himself, covered in sweat.

"Well, how did they get Zeb?" I ask.

"We almost had her, Eva. Binky. She was scared to come with us, but we really almost made it." He sighs. "It doesn't matter now. They're all leaving. The whole caravan. Can't you hear them?"

And it's true. There beyond the walls the lights beam all around, and the sound of what appears to be an army of trucks ricochets off the cobbled stone.

Why would they take Zeb? Where are they even going? "Henry, we have to make a decision here. I mean, I don't think we can outrun those trucks. Some of them are already leaving." I look at him.

The two of us letting this sink in.

"I mean, what are we gonna do? Hurl ourselves onto the

windshields?" I ask him.

The sound of the motors reverberates against the hillside. The lights, a million different floodlights, search down the long winding driveway.

"We need a strategy. Think, Henry. Think!" I am just grasping for straws now.

Henry closes his eyes and I know what he's doing. I keep my mouth shut, hoping somehow in the silence the gears in his brain will start to shift. Maybe there will be a drop, and then another drop, and then a river.

Maybe there will be something, anything, to stop this seemingly endless parade of vehicles down the snaking drive to the sea. As I take in the myriad of white trucks, about twenty of them, I notice a little one at the end. Not white. No, this one is a black truck. And it's not a truck, exactly, but an SUV. And inside the SUV is not a tweedle-guard or an estate sale of oil paintings but a boy. A boy sits in the passenger seat of the mean-looking onyx SUV.

He is looking more grim than I have ever seen him. More troubled than I ever thought he could.

Though his scowl makes him nearly unrecognizable, his blue streaks give him away.

That boy is Zeb.

3

HENRY AND I stand there, our jaws dropped to the ground.

"Eva, do you see what I am seeing?" he asks.

"Yes."

It's hard to tell through the glare off the windshield, but it looks like Binky is in the back seat and Zeb is in the front, both of them bound and gagged. There's a tweedle-guard in the back seat, but there is not a tweedle-guard in the front seat. Nope. In the front seat, driving, is the Midwestern Mastermind.

He watches as the trucks before him pull out in a line. Even from here I can sense his impatience.

"Henry, what are we—"

But before I can finish the sentence I see Henry bounding down the hill, through the foliage, to the loading dock.

"Henry?!"

"Shhh. Eva," he yell-whispers back at me. "I have an idea. Follow me and keep quiet."

So now the two of us are whisper-yelling and running down through the brambles.

"Does it involve teleporting ourselves over to the front gate?" I ask, keenly aware that we have a timing issue.

"That part I haven't figured out yet," he admits. "Here! This way!"

The lights from the panoply of trucks cut across the grass and the road but send everything else into darkness, allowing Henry and I to peer around the corner into the loading dock.

Henry focuses on a little door across the dock.

"There! We need to get in there!" he whispers.

"The utility closet?" I frown.

"Exactly." He turns to me. "All right, I'm going to need you to make a run for it. Listen, Eva, get as far out there as you possibly can."

"But, Henry, how—"

"Eva, I don't care what it takes, just get out there. In front of the very first truck. Do you understand?"

"Yeah, I guess."

Before I can even finish my shrug, he's off bounding toward the utility closet, ducking behind everything there is to be ducked behind. There's so much chaos on the drive out, no one seems to notice. Between the heavy loads of the trucks, the inclement weather, and the mud, this is definitely not the operation our diabolical mastermind envisioned.

To put it bluntly, this thing is moving like molasses.

If the Mastermind was angry to be thirty minutes off schedule, I can't imagine what he's going through now.

As I try to find a path down the hill to somehow get in front of the first truck, I look back and see Henry in a blur, grabbing things off the shelves in the storage closet as if he's suddenly morphed into a tornado. I'm trying to figure out exactly what he's doing but that is not a good thing to be doing while running and . . .

THWAM!

Oh God.

What just happened?

4

IT TAKES ABOUT three seconds for me to actually process all this information. First second, something is wrong. (That was the THWAM.) Second second, I think maybe I just fell. (That was gravity.) Third second, I just fell in something really gross. (Oh, that's mud.)

Yes, ladies and gentlemen of the jury, I just fell face-first in the mud. Yuck. My face is literally covered in it. I have to "de-mud" my eyes to even see out of them. And yes, my mouth, too. What's that taste, you ask? Dirt. That is dirt that I am tasting.

I try to spit the taste out of my mouth, trying not to think about the fact that my mouth, lips, and ears are caked with a combination of rain, dirt, and grass. This is humiliating. Yes, I know, there's no one to see it. But trust me, it's humiliating all the same.

If there are Gods, or angels, or even great programmers in the sky, they are laughing at me right now. That is for sure.

I look up to the heavens.

"Really?! *Really?!*"

But nobody answers me. They all just sit there in their gold thrones, or clouds, or nerd basements in the sky.

I peer through my mud-glasses at Henry. He's bent over something fidgeting. It's impossible to tell what it is but, whatever it is, he's got that look I've seen a million times before.

It's the three-story-marble-run look. The Lego-robot-factory look. Next to him on the ground are the supplies. The materials to his experiment. And I am crossing my fingers.

One of the headlights catches me, and I realize that . . . probably in my new "mud outfit" . . . no one can see me.

Ah!

No one can see me.

The mud! It's like an invisibility cloak!

Down the driveway, making its way through a particularly muddy patch, I see the first truck. It's hard to tell on this giant rolling hill how far it is but, if I were to put it in city terms, I'd say it's about six city blocks down the hill, as the crow flies. So, while they're winding their way through turn after turn on this unnecessarily undulating driveway, I guess I can try running a straight path.

In my mud suit.

Here I go.

5

LOOK, I'VE NEVER been very much of a runner. For instance, in school each spring we have to run the six-hundred-yard dash and I don't mind telling you that is a day I have tried in a myriad of different ways to happen to not be there.

Maybe I have a cold.

Maybe I have a field trip that only I know about.

Maybe I have to study at home for a different test that is really much more important.

Maybe I hit my head and realize I'm actually from another dimension and my name is Zergon from the planet Zlog and my spaceship is waiting down at the lighthouse!

Tried it.

Points for creativity but no dice.

So, you see, every year I end up slogging my way through the six-hundred-yard dash. Dreading it before. Dreading it during. Then, dreading it immediately after for the next year. It's like this one thing that was perfectly designed to make me hate life.

So, that is why, dear friends, the idea of me making a mad dash down what looks like six city blocks, covered in mud, running through mud, is particularly poignant. This is like if you made an egg eat an egg salad. It's full of grimacing, and it's painful to watch.

About a third of the way down the mud I hear a

WHOOSH

whiz by, over my head.

I look up to see whatever it is, but whatever it is, it's traveling at lightning speed and I am traveling at . . . Eva speed. (Don't make fun!)

My dress shoes, which are now just mud shoes, are slipping off my feet with the gloop and the glop of the mud sticking to them and trying to glue my feet to the ground. The fancy dress I picked out just for this wedding occasion is also not exactly improved by the caked-earth look.

Let's face it. I basically just look like a mud monster.

WHOOSH.

Now I hear another mystery item zinging by over my head. But this time, when I look up, I see a streak of light across the sky. Like a mini comet. The comet streaks above my head and soars over all the way to the farthest gate. About a city block in front of the first truck. Whatever the mystery whooshing item is, it sticks into the ground where it lands. Still glowing.

Wait, is that a glow stick?

I pick up the pace, "running" through the gloopy gloppy mud, making my way down the hill toward the glowing item of intrigue.

I have to get there before the first truck. I have to get there before the first truck. Run, Eva, run. Remember Winston. Never, never, never give up.

I can do this.

I

CAN

DO

THIS!

And . . . there goes my shoe in the mud.

Don't worry about it, Eva.

YOU!

CAN!

DO!

THIS!

And . . . there goes my other shoe.

BY THE TIME I make it to the mystery glowing whoosh I have
no idea what I'm supposed to do with it. It's a puzzle I am supposed to put together on the fly. Before the first truck can pass
me, in the mud, in the drizzle, before Zeb and Binky escape
into the night forever.

No pressure.

As I get closer I realize the whooshing was made by some
sort of arrow contraption Henry must have made with a kind of
exploded thing on the back. Like an arrow set off by a chemical
reaction. A rocket arrow? A mini rocket? And I look closer at
the arrow, realizing it's actually the wood part of a plunger.

Oh, Henry.

There seems to be a scribbled note on the side of the plunger/

arrow/rocket. An arrow, with the words written next to it: "Tie us together. Throw at driver. Wait till truck at gate."

"Tie us together?"

I look at the other plunger/arrow/rocket, the first one. Attached to it is a tiny plastic bag filled with something milky and gooey, some sort of liquid. I look at the second plunger/arrow/rocket. Yes, there is a little tiny bag, too, filled with something brownish and oily.

I look back at Henry, all the way up the hill, his silhouette framed in front of the loading dock.

He waves to me. Then gives me the thumbs-up.

I guess this is Henry's way of saying, "You got this."

I take a closer look at the two bags of mystery goo in the plastic baggies. What in the world is in these things?

I look back at Henry.

Another thumbs-up.

Okay, here goes. I tie the two little baggies together. Test it. Making sure it holds tight.

I really hope I don't screw this up, whatever this is.

Gulp.

The first truck seems to have made its way over the last of the muddy patches. Its engine revs and the blinding lights begin turning toward me, there, at the very end of the driveway, just to the side of the gate. I'm squatting down like a mud creature, just two eyes staring down the glowing eyes of the truck.

It's me against you now, truck.

Wait.

Wait.

Wait . . .

The truck is coming toward me now, the momentum of the hill speeding it up. It almost looks for a second to be slipping in the mud but then it rights itself, barreling down the driveway.

It crosses my mind now that if, say, I don't manage to throw this mystery plastic baggie combo and if, say, I don't manage to hit the driver's side with it . . . this truck could very likely barrel straight down the hill smack-dab into me. Little old mud rock me just sitting by the side of the road.

Wait.

Wait.

Barreling truck.

Barreling truck.

Wait.

And . . .

WHOOOOOOOOSSSHHH.

There it goes.

7

THERE ARE ONLY so many things a mysterious gooey liquid combo trapped in plastic baggies can do. I mean, it's not like it's going to hit the front windshield and turn into a chicken. Or fly up into the air and turn into a spaceship.

But what it actually does is just right.

Because what this baby actually does do, upon impact, is explode.

BOOOOM!

As soon as the plastic baggie combo makes impact with the windshield it ignites, setting off a kaboom that sets off a series of precise and exquisite events, each one leading to the next in perfect combination. Like a Rube Goldberg contraption.

First, the driver freaks the heck out at the blast, jumping

three feet into the air. Maybe four.

Second, he loses control of the steering wheel because he happens to be three feet in the air.

Third, the truck, now left to its own devices sans steering wheel, loses control and begins to go off the edge of the driveway.

Fourth, the wheels of the truck, now off the driveway, go sloshing through the mud, now taking the truck farther into chaos.

Fifth, the wheels of the front of the truck get stuck, but the wheels of the back of the truck are still wanting to move forward.

And sixth, beautifully sixth, the back of the truck comes forward, essentially jackknifing the truck across the driveway and blocking it for any of the other trucks.

So, let's say, if you were the Midwestern Mastermind, sitting in the back of the line of giant white trucks, impatiently waiting, what you would see is a giant explosion up front, a crash, and a resulting white semitruck strewn across the road in just the precise way to make it impossible for any of the other trucks to get by it.

Genius.

I look back up the hill at Henry, who is standing there in the distance, proud.

I shake my head. Whatever that was, and however that happened, I am in awe.

We look at each other and I pretend bow.

What? I'm part of this, too, you know. I'm the one who threw that mystery plastic baggie combo, risking life and limb. Lest we forget.

I could really dance a jig right now, even in my mud costume.

But there is a new issue.

As I look up the driveway I see the skinny but rapidly growing figure of a man who has a face the color of a lobster and steam coming out of his ears.

I can't dance a jig now. I will have to dance a jig later. Right now all I can do is slowly, casually step backward, crouching down with each step to become one with the earth again. A kind of primordial reverse of Darwin's evolution. I am coming back from whence I came. Back into the mud and the mire, back to my life as a single-cell amoeba!

The Midwestern Mastermind doesn't even stop his momentum down the long, flooded hill. He just keeps going full tilt the entire way down and then flings himself at the driver.

"Are you allergic to success?!"

The driver looks up at him, dazed from the accident. "Wh-what?"

"Do you hate money? Are you an idiot? What the heck happened?!!"

The driver's eyes roll back into his head.

And he promptly faints.

8

I HAVE TO hand it to Henry. Not only did he just launch a plunger into the air like it was a bow and he was Robin Hood, he created an exploding chemical reaction, thereby jackknifing a semitruck . . . and as a result caused one heck of a distraction.

Every single truck driver has opened their doors to come out and take a gander at the crash, the truck, and the sight of the Midwestern Mastermind hopping around like a deranged chicken. It is now that I realize I never quite understood the expression "hopping mad." Seeing the Mastermind, not thirty feet away, flailing his arms like a rabid seagull while hopping from one foot to the other has really solidified it for me.

I get clips of the words, through the rain, which has now

picked up, of course. Gone is the drizzle and now back to cats and dogs it is!

"You . . . fnjrefinfejfi! I can't believe . . . iafifihfu! This is the most . . . ijafiirrg!" He squawks from the side of the driveway, the truck driver leaning away from his bile and possible spit.

He hops again. "It's like I hired the Marx Brothers!"

At this the actual Marx brothers appear behind him. In ghostly form.

One of them, Groucho, winks at me. "I resemble that remark."

He billows in front of me, puffing on his cigar.

"Um. Not that I mean to sound ungrateful. Or uncharmed. Because I am. But what, exactly, are you doing here?" I ask.

"What are we doing here? What are you doing here?! I mean, have you looked at yourself in the mirror?"

He does have a point there.

"Okay, okay. Yes, this is not one of my better looks." I shrug.

"Look, it's no good just sitting there like a lump on a bog. I mean a bump on a log." He waves his cigar.

Behind him, down the road, the sound of muffled swear words continue.

Groucho leans in. "No, sir. You gotta fight, gotta get up and fight. Why look at me! I've worked myself up from nothing to a state of extreme poverty!"

I can't help smiling.

"No, sir, you gotta get up! Get up and get up there and help your brother before he turns into a clam!" he exclaims.

I brush the mud off me.

Groucho is right. There's enough distraction down here for a while.

"But how should I—"

I turn back to Groucho and his brothers. But they have disappeared into the pouring rain. The only thing left is the faint smell of cigar smoke wafting through the air.

9

HALFWAY UP THE muddy hill I realize I don't see Henry. I mean, yes, it was his ingenious plan to crash the truck at the bottom of the hill and, yes, he had given me the thumbs-up gesture from high above my muddy ditch, but since Groucho and his gang showed up, he seems to have disappeared.

Up up up the hill I climb, still covered in mud, still camouflaged . . . now not only by the mud but by the firelit chaos behind me. At one point I look back at the Midwestern Mastermind and his tweedles, trying and failing to dislodge one of the tires. Yes, I am proud of my work. I stand there, looking down at them as they grumble.

"I did that."

Small solace to a mud-covered girl in the rain but, hey, you have to take it where you can get it.

I keep expecting Henry to pop out from somewhere up on the landing dock, but he is nowhere to be found.

At this point, I'm wondering what, exactly, I should be doing. Yes, I need to find the black SUV with Zeb and Binky. This, I understand. But Groucho told me to help my brother!

Hopefully, I can find Henry and he will have already invented another genius scheme. Otherwise, I will definitely have to put my thinking cap on.

Passing the line of trucks up the driveway is a bit surreal. Every truck door is open, some of them even blinking, one with a constant *ding ding ding*. Each driver has abandoned his post, fled down the hill to somehow get that jackknifed truck out of the driveway. I shake my head. I gotta hand it to Henry.

"Pssst! Eva!" The urgent whisper comes from behind a willow acacia to my right, up the slope.

"Henry! Wow. Do you see this?" I gesture down the hill at the chaotic scene below. "I mean, you have really outdone yourself."

Henry takes a bit of pride in his work. "Yes, I must say, that was more satisfying than I could have imagined. I wasn't quite sure the alkaline lithium from the batteries would mix with the water at impact, so, yes, that was extremely fulfilling."

"Is that what that was? You made that from batteries you found in the utility closet? Oh, Henry. That was inspired!"

He turns red, sheepish, and now decides he's more comfortable just changing the subject altogether.

"Eva, I think the black SUV reversed down the servant's entrance, due to the inclement weather. I'm not certain if there's an exit that way but if there is—"

"Zeb!" I crash in over Henry, spotting the SUV in the distance, heading in the exact opposite direction as the truck debacle.

"Is it possible there's a back entrance? But that's impossible. I'm fairly certain the only entrance is down the driveway. In fact, we are on a mountain." He thinks. "Unless . . ."

"Unless what?" I ask.

"Unless . . . there's a . . . secret passageway?" Henry turns to look at the headlights of the SUV making their way toward the mountain in the downpour.

"No, there can't be." I look. Following the lights of the black SUV.

"Perhaps that is where the rest of the minions are meant to escape. The ones left guarding the wedding guests," he suggests.

The two of us look up to the arched windows of the wedding chapel. The warm glow emitted gives no hint to the down-and-dirty hostage situation within. In fact, you could easily see that from the road and think, "Awww . . . they're having some sort of nighttime service."

Henry keeps his eyes on the onyx SUV winding its way up the side of the mountain.

"If there is a path there, it's definitely not in the guidebooks," Henry notes.

"If there is a path there . . . I definitely don't see it. Do you?"

"No, Eva. No, I positively do not. A passage through the mountain, the engineering alone would cost millions." He thinks.

We look at each other.

"Well, it's not like Hearst didn't *have millions*." I say the obvious.

"Point taken," he admits.

Our eyes stay mesmerized by the SUV, now looking like a beetle with lights, finding its way in the distance. It's getting farther and farther away but even in this deluge, I feel like I can almost make out a trace of a little boy in the passenger seat.

A boy with a mop of blond hair, painted in blue.

10

THE FIRST TIME Henry came home with his new friend, I didn't know what to make of it. I didn't know what to do.

If my parents were alive, which is something I find I say to myself more times than I care to admit, they would say I should do zero. Nothing. Just be myself. Exist. And let Zeb exist alongside us and see how it goes.

My mother would have opened her arms to Zeb just as she has opened her arms to everyone from Chattanooga to Timbuktu. My father probably would have tried to engage Zeb in conversation about the Dodgers, the Lakers, the LA River project, or any other topic that he could dig out from his giant brain that would put Zeb at ease. Not that Zeb needs to be put any more at ease. If he was any more at ease he would melt into the surf.

As it was, no one was home but the three of us kids and Marisol, so I chose to meet Zeb with a certain amount of caution.

However, after weeks and weeks of watching Henry and Zeb, Zeb and Henry, building a two-story Lego supercomplex, complete with irrigation system, outlet mall, and furniture store called "Furniture R Us," I decided that Zeb was all right in my book. Even if he was from the dreaded and somehow irritating Los Angeles.

Of course, as months went by, it became clear from all of our interactions that maybe my earlier view of his birthplace was a little . . . close-minded?

It was a moment of self-reflection. My parents would not have been proud.

As Zeb's dad became more and more involved with his betrothed, Binky, it seemed like Zeb was over at our house about forty percent of his life. Which was fine with us. Henry liked having him around. Henry liked him.

And I liked him. Despite not wanting to. Despite myself.

In fact, I kind of came to see him as a sort of secret little brother, a happy-go-lucky one. So now I had not one but two kid brothers to worry about. But there was still something, some unnamed thing, that irked me. Something that tended to flare up every now and again. Something I couldn't explain.

Again, sometimes I think I don't really understand feelings.

So, the point of this is . . . watching Zeb being spirited away up the hill in the torrential downpour is like watching a black SUV drive away with Henry's arm, or his toe, or his heart.

And no one gets a piece of my brother. No one.

11

"HENRY, WE HAVE to do something! We can't just stand here while Zeb is whisked away to God knows where—"

"Yes, yes. I'm thinking. I'm thinking," Henry replies.

But before he can finish I see something and have decided on my own plan of action.

"Follow me!" I tell him, heading toward the far end of the loading dock.

"What? What are we doing exactly?" Henry asks.

"The golf carts! We are stealing a golf cart," I answer.

"We are?"

There's a row of white golf carts in the corner. Five, to be exact. Of course, the keys are nowhere to be found.

"Keys, keys, keys, keys. If I were the keys, where would I be?" I'm talking to myself.

"Probably in . . ." Henry looks around and then points. "There."

He's pointing inside a sort of mini office there tucked into the loading dock. Yes, that is exactly where I would be if I were a key.

"Okay, you get in. I'll grab the keys." I run into the tiny office, scrambling through the papers and ledgers, some motor oil, and a few hot-rod calendars.

"Wait? Does this mean I'm driving?" Henry calls out.

"Yes!" I answer. *Scramble scramble scramble.* Behind the motor oil? No. Under this biblical pile of receipts? No. In this metal desk? No. Think think think. Ah! There, the closet.

"I'm not sure if I'm very good at driving!" Henry yells out.

"I'm sure you're fine. When was the last time you tried it?" Yes, there. Inside the closet door. A row of keys.

There are only about fifty of them.

Ugh.

"The last time I drove?"

"Yeah," I say, grabbing the keys.

"I believe that would be . . . never," Henry adds.

I look at him. Okay, this is not good.

"Well, we'll cross that bridge when we come to it. Try this key." I hand him a silver one.

"No."

"This one." It has a red tag attached.

"No."

"What about this one?" This one has a blue tag attached.

"Not even close."

I hand him a smaller, gold one. "How about this?"

"No."

"This?" That one has a black rubber thing around it.

"There must be a more efficient way to do this."

"Do you know how to hot-wire a golf cart?" I ask.

"Most assuredly not," he answers.

"Then keep looking." I hand him a smaller silver one.

"This one?"

"I think we already tried that one." He squints.

"Okay, this one."

"Wait. Waaaa . . . aaait." He hesitates a moment and . . .
Click.

The key turns.

The engine starts.

"It's working!" I leap in the air.

"Yes! Small problem. I don't know how to drive." Henry
dampens the mood.

"Well, haven't you played like a video game or something
where you're supposed to be driving a race car or something?"
I ask.

"Video game?" Henry looks at me. "Have you met . . . me?"

And he's right. Our parents never let him play video games.
Except sometimes *Minecraft.*

"If you want me to build you a ferromagnetic fluid reaction, well, see exhibit A." He points back down the hill at the tangle of trucks. "But steering an actual vehicle? In analog? I don't think so."

"Fine. Scooch over."

"Is that really the best solution?" Henry ponders.

"We have to do something! And this is the only game in town."

"Fine. But I must insist you wear your seat belt." He secures his own with a *click*.

"Fine."

I fasten mine. *Click*.

And then yes, okay, I hit the gas a little too hard and the two of us go careening forward, nearly clipping the bumper of one of the remaining golf carts. I admit it. Henry screams.

"No, I've got it. I've got it," I say.

But I so don't have it.

We are lurching forward up the back service driveway, slippery road beneath us, careening this way and that.

After a moment of silence, Henry pipes up.

"I can't believe you said that."

"What?" I say, trying to concentrate on the road.

"The only game in town," he answers.

"What's wrong with that?" I swerve to not hit a tree.

"It's just so unlike you."

"What do you mean?" I swerve to not hit another tree.

"It just sounds a bit . . . contrived." He thinks.

"Contrived?! We're about to steer off this roadway into the abyss and you are calling my language contrived?!" I swerve to not hit a rock, then overcorrect, nearly steering us off the road.

"I'm just saying it didn't feel quite genuine," he adds.

"Genuine?! I *genuinely* believe I am risking my life and limbs here, and yours, too, now that I think of it, trying to rescue *your* friend who showed up one day and just sort of oozed into our lives and became like the most important person in your world! Which is irksome—especially when I *genuinely* believe that very *first* most important person to you was always . . . *me*! *So* I would appreciate it if you saved your linguistic and driving criticism and instead thanked me for helping this total random stranger who seems to have totally eclipsed me!"

This just sits there for a moment. Both of us in silence.

Henry bites the inside of his lip.

"Eva? . . . Thank you," he utters.

The rain is pouring down now, pounding the top of the golf cart in buckets.

Henry stays silent.

"Don't do that!" I yell.

"What?"

"That!"

"That what?" he asks.

"That silent treatment!" I burst.

"I'm merely trying to facilitate a successful journey," he comments.

And he's right. There's no reason to be having this heated interaction right now, but somehow I can't stop myself. It would take an act of God to change my train of thought, but luckily, or unluckily, an act of God is exactly what happens.

12

IT'S A FLASH of light. A flash of light followed by a thunderous *CRACK* so loud it shakes the ground. At first, I don't know what it is. I'm not used to lightning. It's not like this is Tornado Alley or Santa Fe or any of those other places where the jet stream comes down from the arctic and gusts into the warm air from the gulf, creating fantastic weather systems, lightning storms and twisters you can see breaking out over the plains.

This is California. Lightning is an *event*. A precious offering. A gift. And, in this case, maybe a curse.

Why is it a curse? Because when said lightning struck, not thirty feet away from little ol' us in our tiny white golf cart, I might possibly have hydroplaned off the road and slid this little white golf cart about twenty feet through the mud. . . .

"AHHHHHHHH!!!!" Henry screams that way.

"EEEEEEEEEEEE!!!" I scream this way.

. . . over the brambles . . .

"AHHHHHHHH!!!!"

"EEEEEEEEEEEE!!!"

. . . over this bump . . .

"AHHHHHHHH!!!!"

"EEEEEEEEEEEE!!!"

. . . and that bump . . .

"AHHHHHHHH!!!!"

"EEEEEEEEEEEE!!!"

. . . and, thankfully, by-the-grace-of-God-ingly, up *just* a tad at the very bitter end where the base of an enormous craggy oak tree forms a kind of gentle slope, thereby permitting us to . . . not die.

Even though this whole process takes about fifty seconds it feels like fifty hours slowed down, every detail, every bramble, every bump, every piece of mud flying. Even the look between Henry and me in the midst of it. Each of our faces containing the same expression, "Are we gonna die right now?" That split-second look, that hydroplane moment, all of it seeming to take the time of an entire movie.

And I will never forget it.

The engine whines to a stop. Henry and I sit there, stunned. Neither of us says anything as neither of us, I'm pretty sure, can actually believe we made it out of that one alive. Inside my chest, my heart is lurching to get out. *Thump thump. Thump thump. Thump thump.*

And then.

"Eva, are we alive?" Henry asks.

I look around, trying to get my bearings.

"I think so." I exhale.

"Prove it," he says.

"What do you mean?" I ask.

"Pinch me?" He looks at me.

I shrug. Then pinch him.

"*Ow!*" He winces. "Definitely not the afterlife."

But we're not mad at each other. Oh, no. Not now. Not after we just almost met our maker in the mud off a Central Coast mountain.

"Come to think of it, it's not the worst place to die," Henry muses.

"What?"

"I mean. Hearst Castle. In a car chase . . . It's kind of glamourous. Plus, I suppose we'd get to spend time with all those other famous ghosts. A kind of macabre festival . . ." He rolls it over in his mind.

"There's nothing glamourous about dying, Henry!" I unfasten my seat belt. "I just thank God I had the good sense to insist we wear our seat belts!"

Henry rolls his eyes.

The two of us are trying to get out of what feels like a giant mud pit. It's more complicated than it would seem.

Henry looks up the road.

"I doubt if we'll catch up with them now," he admits.

I follow his gaze. At this point, I don't even see any headlights.

"I don't get it. How could they get over the mountain? Or through the mountain? There's no road there," I ponder.

Henry thinks. "Do you think it's possible they simply stopped? Perhaps waiting?"

"Waiting for what?"

"Perhaps they are waiting for . . . the Midwestern Mastermind. Perhaps he told his tweedle-guards to take Binky and Zeb away until he's completed his diabolical heist."

"So, you think they might just be up there, like . . . chillaxing?'" I ask.

He blinks. "Yes. It's a possibility. That they are up there. *Chillaxing.*"

"Well, if that's the case . . . what if we . . . I don't know . . . tried to sneak up on them?"

"They have one guard as I recall," Henry says. "Is that what you recall?"

"Yes, Henry. That's what I recall."

"I think it advisable we formulate a plan before we make any attempt to make contact," he decides.

"Yes. Definitely. Wonder powers . . . formulate."

Henry leans up against the side of the crashed golf cart, smeared with mud, and closes his eyes in thought.

"Eva?" He opens one eye.

"Yeah?"

"I feel the need to tell you that you are irreplaceable. No one. Not Zeb. Not anyone, can replace you. I'm . . . I'm saddened you would think that."

He looks at me.

"It's just . . . it all happened so fast. And he's so perfect. And fun. And interesting. And mellow. And he thinks you're sooooo coooooooool." My stomach twists.

"Yes. But he's not a sister replacement."

"A sister replacement?"

"Yes. You have to order them. They ship from Tokyo. Yours is coming in three years. The Sister 3000. It lights up," he teases.

"Oh, Henry." I walk over to him, wading through the mud. I hug him. He hugs me back.

"Eva?"

"Yeah?"

"You know that we're basically mud people right now."

"Yes. Yes we are."

The hum of the truck interrupts our moment.

From this little mud pit/golf cart crash site, we can see down the hill to the two distinct towers of Hearst Castle, looking a bit like two beige honeycombs spiraling up into the night. Down below, more difficult to see through the rain, the row of trucks winds down the hill toward the ocean.

I notice that the lights of some of the trucks are on. That's not a good sign. They were all off, at a standstill, before. I peer farther, trying to make out the very first truck, at the bottom of the hill. It's impossible to see at first but then it slowly comes into focus. The first truck. And the truck behind it. And the other trucks, too.

"Henry?"

"Yes, Sister 3000?"

"They're moving."

He looks at me, blank.

"The trucks back at the castle." I gesture down the hill. "The trucks are moving."

13

DO WE GET the art or do we get the Zeb?

"Henry, what do we do?" I'm so confused.

"Well, it really depends. Do we value thousands of years of precious art and artifacts? Or do we value the priceless nature of friendship . . . of humanity? And if we do value material things more, then what does that make us? What have we allowed ourselves to—?"

"Henry!" I roll my eyes.

"Okay, let's go get Zeb," he acquiesces.

As if to jolt us back to life a light strikes me across the face.

"Wait. What?"

I turn toward the light and see it's coming in a beam through the trees.

"Henry! Look. Headlights!" I point.

He peers into the headlights, coming from the distance down the hill toward us.

"They're turned around! They're coming back!" he gasps.

"Do you think it's them? Binky and Zeb?" I ask.

"I hope it's them," he exclaims. "Here. Help me. Hurry!"

I follow him up toward the road, the scene of our fateful golf cart crash.

"Grab as many rocks and branches as you can. Here! Grab that one." Henry is already in action, grabbing everything he can lift from the brambles and hurling it toward the road. "We have to create a de facto blockade!"

The headlights of the SUV swing this way and that through the chaparral, making it impossible to tell exactly how close they are or how much time we have.

"That! Yes, that branch there. That's perfect." He chucks it on the road. It lands with a thud.

"What if it crashes and it hurts Zeb? Or Binky? Or even the guard for that matter, I mean, I don't want to be violent," I say, considering.

"Eva. This is all we have. This is it." And then he looks up, making fun of me. "It's the *only game in town.*"

I roll my eyes.

"You're never gonna let that go, are you?"

"Probably not." He continues grabbing and hurling.

"Well, you know, not everybody can be cool *all the time.* I mean, sometimes you just say something." Grab. Hurl. Grab. Hurl.

The lights seem to be brighter now, then gone, then brighter, then gone, as the SUV winds its way down the road.

"We need more rocks. Eva, rocks!"

"Wait, did you just say that Eva rocks?" I smile.

He sighs. "Fine. Eva rocks! Now give me some rocks!" he barks.

"Here." I hurl a rock at the road. "And here. And here."
Thud. Thud. Thud.

The roadway has not the best blockade across it, but a sizable one. There's possibly enough debris to put a wrench in their works.

"I hope this works," I whisper.

"I don't understand," he whispers back.

"What?"

"I don't understand why they would be coming back."

"Maybe . . ." I think. "Maybe the Midwestern Mastermind gave them the signal. Like 'We're leaving now, it's all clear. Let's complete this heist.'"

"But why wouldn't they just wait back at the castle? It doesn't make sense," he ponders.

"Maybe there was something up there. Like a hidden treasure. Or a key. Or maybe even a secret code," I offer.

The lights are brighter now and the sound of the engine gets louder as it makes its way down toward us, twisting and turning on the switchbacks.

"I can't take it."

"Take what?" Henry asks.

"The suspense. It's killing me."

Henry gives me a look.

"No, seriously. Like is the SUV going to crash? How good is the driver? These tweedle-guards don't really seem to know what they're doing, quite frankly. I mean, maybe Zeb like convinced the guard to seek the right path or whatever, like he did the Redondo guy."

"'Seek the right path or whatever,'" Henry quotes me.

"You know what I mean. Zeb has like magic powers or something."

Now the engine is getting louder, louder. Now the SUV is getting closer, closer, closer . . .

SCREEEEEEEEEEEEEEEEEE

EEEEEEE

EEEEEEEEEECH.

THUD.

Henry and I look at each other.

That sounded bad.

14

I BET THE trees around here are wondering what all these car accidents are all about. I bet they're talking to one another right now through their underground networks of roots and fungi, saying things like, "Um, did you guys notice there have been two screeching vehicle crashes aboveground in the past hour?"

The oaks and the paloverde and the sycamores all nodding in agreement. "Yes, indeed. Tough night." The cacti doing a face-palm. The quivering aspens shuddering.

It's hard to tell what just happened exactly. First there was a *screech*, then there was a *scritch*, then there was a loud, prolonged *klaaklacklacklack thumpthumthump* followed by the final aforementioned pronounced *THUD*.

In the brambles about twenty feet down the road, the SUV has crashed. Our plan "worked . . . ?" The SUV tilts slightly to the side, headlights still on, with one of the rear wheels spinning, futile, in the open air.

Henry and I watch in stunned silence as the driver's side door opens up. Then a hand reaches out, pushing the door again, and lugging its body behind it. Neither the hand nor the body belong to Zeb. Or Binky.

In fact, both the hand and the body belong to one of the tweedle-guards. He tweedles around to the back and opens that door, which appears to be a bit stuck, thereby letting out Binky with a grunt. His grunt. Not her grunt. She just looks dazed and confused.

Henry and I share a look. Where is Zeb?

But that question is immediately answered when we see him climb out of the slanted driver's side as well, looking the opposite of dazed and confused, and actually thrilled.

"Okay, that was awesome." Zeb checks to make sure all his limbs are working. "Not a scratch!"

Henry and I look at each other. You can't help smiling. There could be a category-five hurricane overhead and Zeb would say, "Wow, look at that eye! What a miracle!"

Binky is looking around, beginning to get her bearings.

"Where are we?" she asks, rubbing her neck.

"Shh. Keep quiet," the tweedle-guard barks, making his way around the SUV, assessing the damage.

"We caught air!" Zeb says, proud.

"I said quiet. Stay here." The tweedle-guard grumbles his way over to the road. "Darn it."

I guess he's not happy about this little wrench in the works.

Henry tries to get Zeb's attention with a bird sound.

"Kaw-KAW!"

I look at him. That was such a bad bird sound.

"KeKAW KeKAW!" My bird sound is impeccable.

Zeb looks up. Thinks. Starts looking around.

"It's working," I whisper. "KeKAW KeKAW!"

And now Henry, "Kaw KAW! Kaw KAW!"

"Sh. They're going to think there's too many birds," I whisper-yell.

"There's just the right amount of birds. There's not a single bird too many." And then, in defiance, "Kaw KAW Kaw KAW!"

Not to be outdone, I correct him. "KeKAW KeKAW!"

"Kaw KAW! Kaw KAW!"

"KeKAW KeKAW!"

Zeb's head pokes in through the brambles. "What the heck are you guys doing? You sound like a den of mutant frog-chickens!"

"Zeb, oh my God. Are you okay?" I gasp.

"Under the circumstances?" He thinks. "Pretty good, actually."

"How's Binky?" Henry asks.

Zeb contemplates. "Honestly, I think she's kind of in a state of shock."

"What do we do about the guard?" I ask. "Is he nice like the other guy, that Redondo one?"

"Nope," Zeb replies. "I'd say he's more in the I-might've-spent-time-in-prison, I-might-not-care-if-I-go-back kind of mode."

"A career criminal." Henry's take.

"Yeah. Also not the brightest bulb on the dashboard," Zeb informs us.

"Hmm."

"Like now, for instance. He's just looking at the road." The three of us take a look at the tweedle-guard. He's walking around the sight of the crash, scratching his head.

"I think this might call for a good old-fashioned outsmarting, Henry," I suggest.

"Hmm. I suppose. Let's see." Henry starts pondering. You can practically see the workers in his brain leafing through the catalogue. That? No. This? No. Maybe that? Possibly.

Then the voice of the tweedle-guard.

"Hey, where'd that kid go?" he grunts out, staccato.

"I'm sorry. What?" Binky is really in her own little world.

"The blue hair kid. Where is he?" Another grunt.

"I'm . . ." Binky looks around. "I'm not sure . . ."

"Ugh!" he snaps. "I hate this job!"

The tweedle-guard stomps into the bushes.

It's hard to make out his shape through the brambles, but the sound of his grunts does seem to be getting louder.

Henry, Zeb, and I stare at one another, a trio of frozen mud statues.

15

WE WHISPER TO one another, mud statues in the brush.

"We have to do something!" I suggest.

"Yes. I know," Henry whispers.

"Maybe like soon," Zeb suggests.

"Yes, I get it," Henry replies.

"Maybe like . . ." Zeb looks up. "Right now."

The three of us look up. The tweedle-guard is just round the paloverde tree. Our only camouflage.

"Henry?" I whisper.

But it's too late. The guard steps beyond the paloverde and the three of us look up in the headlights like three blind mice. Caught.

"Um. Hi!" That is my brilliant reply.

"What are you kids doing here?!" he grumbles. "Never mind. Forget it. Come with me."

The three of us hesitate.

"Come on. Trust me. You don't want to try my patience right now. Lord."

He has a point here. He is a big guy. And he seems to be missing a neck. Also, his arms are as big as my legs. And he definitely seems like he's at the end of his rope.

Henry makes an attempt. "If I may be so bold, I would like to point out that potentially the fastest way down the mountain—"

"Shut up, kid." He cuts him off. "I'm tryin' to help—"

Clang!

This tweedle is on the floor. And standing over him, tire iron in hand, is—

Binky.

16

BINKY TWIRLS THE tire iron like a baton.

"You didn't think I had it in me, did you?"

Despite the hair filled with brambles, dirt on her face, and wedding dress in tatters, she actually looks kind of adorable. And dangerous. But like, in a girl-power way.

"Wooooow. Binky." Zeb lights up. "Nice job!"

Indeed, it is a nice job. Binky stands there, contemplating the fallen tweedle-guard at our feet.

"Wait. Okay, so you just . . . bonked that guy on the head?" I ask.

"It appears so," Henry responds.

"Was he starting to say something about helping?" I ask.

"Helping my foot. That man had me hostage! He would

have done the same to you!" Binky looks down at him. "Is he dead?"

Now, we all look down at him.

"Hmm." Henry bends down, investigating. "His chest is moving. So, he is breathing. That's the good news. The bad news is he could wake up at any second."

"Yeah, we should probably bail," Zeb suggests.

Binky takes the lead.

"Kids, I have a plan."

Binky has . . . *a plan*!

You know, I may be guilty of pegging her as a "damsel in distress" type. As it turns out, she's quite capable. Perhaps even formidable.

"Binky. Thank you for saving our hides. We definitely owe you one," I tell her.

"Aw, you kids. You think I'm going to cool my heels while this big oaf lays his big oaf hands on you? No way. No, sir." She winks, a twinkle in her eye.

"C'mon. I think we can make it down to the chapel if we hurry," Zeb urges.

"Oh, no. I have a better plan," Binky pipes up.

"What do you have in mind?" Henry asks.

Binky hefts the tire iron over her shoulder. "Follow me."

As we approach the line of trucks, it's obvious a kind of "second path" has been created by some of the minions, who have placed a series of wooden pallets over the ditch and through the mud. Very inventive. Some of the trucks have actually been able to make their way through the mud and out into whatever underground art-thievery scene they had programmed into their GPS.

The Mastermind stands there, observing each truck go out into the misty night, peeking in the back, cataloguing, paying the drivers, giving a final nod. Taking in the whole scene, it is clear this is really a solo operation. He's the brains. They're the muscle. This explains why the pay is so horrible. This is a winner-take-all situation.

It's baffling how people can be so greedy. I mean, here is this guy, only able to do this on the backs of this tweedle-army, and yet they are making peanuts compared to him. It's not as if they won't go to jail if they are caught. Or perhaps even turn on him, if the police start sniffing around them at some point. See. It's just bad management. Where's the positive mental attitude, the loyalty, the motivation?

But maybe this is his Achilles' heel?

This uber-greed?

Gosh there are *so many trucks*. So many . . .

The synapses in my head begin to fire, but just as they are about to form an actual thought, the process is interrupted.

"So, what's the plan, Binks?" Zeb asks.

Binky looks up. "Excuse me?"

"What's the plan? You know, to take the serpent's head or whatever?" Zeb asks, a bit winded by our hike down the mountain.

"Don't worry. I have it all figured out. You're going to love it." Binky elbows him, chiding.

Zeb smiles, but Henry is not convinced.

"I don't mean to sound rude, but wouldn't it be better if we all knew the plan? So we could aid in its enactment?" Henry asks.

"You're right. I see what you mean." Binky pauses. "Okay, wait. Here. See these rocks? You kids stay here and I'll give you the signal."

"The signal for what?" Zeb yells, but Binky's already jogged ahead.

Then I have a thought again, or the beginnings of a thought. The thought stretches its many arms and fingers around my brain and is just about to wriggle itself into position.

The thought is: *Yes, there's going to be a twenty-course meal . . . because this wedding is so elaborate. I mean, just remember those gazillions of trucks parking before the wedding . . . you know, those trucks you noticed right before the ceremony?*

And then the thought veered like this:

Wait a minute. Who called those trucks in the first place? Well, obviously, it was the Midwestern Mastermind because this is all his diabolical plan. Except did he just cancel all of Binky's wedding plans and call his own people? How would he even do that? I mean, did he sit there and research all of Binky's wedding arrangements? Was he the wedding planner? Um, no. Definitely not. I specifically remember Zeb saying the wedding planner was a guy named Fabio who wore an ascot.

Then the thought veered this way:

Someone had to tell the Midwestern Mastermind all the details of this wedding. But who would have known them all . . . ?

I gasp.

Binky.

I turn to Zeb and Henry. "Guys, this is an inside job! We have to get out of here!"

"You kids aren't going anywhere." And in that moment, we are surrounded. By Binky, who is slapping the heavy tire iron in a slow rhythm into her palm, and a circle of beefy tweedle-guards.

Ladies and gentleman of the jury, let it be known here and from this point onward:

Binky is in cahoots with the Midwestern Mastermind!

"Binky?" Zeb says it, his body a deflated balloon. "This was . . . you?"

"How could you?" Henry is more affronted than anything. "I took your side!"

Binky looks at me, as if it's my turn.

"Binky," I say. "Is that even your real name?"

"Of course not," she scoffs.

"Well, what is it?"

"None of your beeswax."

"I know what it is," Zeb looks up, a moment of truth.

She finally looks back at him. "What?"

He does the L sign on his forehead. "LOSE-ER."

She tilts her head. "Very amusing."

"Your name is LOSER!"

"Yeah. yeah. Say it all you want, kid. Because in the next few minutes this LOSER"—she puts the L on her own forehead now—"is about to win."

17

"I CAN'T BELIEVE this whole thing with my dad was a cover for a heist!" Zeb grumbles. "That's just cold. Only an unfeeling monster could manipulate someone like—"

"I'm right here," Binky responds, finishing up the ties around his back.

Yep, you heard me. Zeb is now completely tied up to a chair. As is Henry. As am I. It's a chair-tie party.

Zeb goes on. "It's as if somewhere in her past she just lost that piece of her, the piece that knows how to love and care, the piece that gives us all our humanity . . . the piece called a . . . heart."

"Um, like I said. Right here," Binky replies.

"'For what doth it profit a man, if he gain the whole world, and suffer the loss of his own soul?' Matthew 16:26," Henry intones.

"Tell her, Henry! BAM! That's some biblical stuff. In your face, Binkster!" Zeb celebrates.

"All right, that's it." Binky slaps a piece of tape over his mouth.

I could easily help him continue his quote except I, too, have a mouth full of tape.

Side note: Tape is not a good taste. It's somewhere between wallpaper and glue. With hints of rubbing alcohol. Long on the tongue.

"Now you snooty brats stay where you are! Because Mitch and I—"

"Who's Mitch?" Henry asks.

"Why, the man helping me execute this brilliant plan of mine," Binky answers.

So. The truth is revealed. The Midwestern Mastermind isn't actually the mastermind behind this heist at all. The whole time, the actual mastermind has been the bride herself.

She hovers over Henry's mouth with a final mouth-size piece of tape. "But, wait!" he shouts. "Eva said she saw you crying!"

"Oh, I have wept today, tiny nerd boy. I have cried tears of sheer joy over how well my diabolical plan has proceeded! It really is a thing of beauty. You must admit it. What bride purposely sabotages her own wedding?"

Henry is about to respond, but Binky presses the tape over

his lips, finishing off with a *pat pat pat*. "Now I won't have to worry about a single one of you . . . ever again!" Her shoulders begin to shake. She gulps in a breath. *Sob.* Salty streaks flow from the corners of her eyes. "I am just . . . so . . . good at this!" She walks toward the door. "Tah!" she calls over her shoulder before sealing the door shut.

I finally have a chance to look around. It appears that we are in a combination basement/cave. A basecave. Some of the walls are stone. And some are rock. Bedrock, I'm assuming. Okay, we must be under the castle somewhere. The door is a wood door, with black metal fixtures, wrought iron. It looks like it was probably constructed in the twenties. Sturdy. They don't make them like that anymore.

As the door rattles to a close, the three of us find ourselves looking at one another with tape covering our mouths, eyes wide.

Henry is scrunching his mouth and his jaw this way and that to get the tape to somehow come off.

I wonder how long they plan on keeping us in here. Is this just until after the heist? But then, how will anyone even know we're here? I start looking around the basecave. Is there even any ventilation in here? I mean, I don't see any vents.

That's not good.

Henry keeps wriggling his mouth. Now Zeb and I are trying it, too. Wriggle wriggle wriggle. Wriggle wriggle wriggle.

I manage to wriggle half the tape off my mouth. Thank God!

I tell myself to definitely not think about the possibility of a finite amount of oxygen down here. Nope, not thinking about that. Definitely not.

Zeb's tape is falling off now, too. Somehow Henry's seems to be stuck tighter. Maybe it was the extra pats at the end.

I figure prayer isn't a bad idea at a time such as this, so I formulate one. It goes, "Please, great creator above, Vishnu, Krishna, Yahweh, or whatever great creator spirit you actually are . . . please help us!"

Nothing happens.

Zeb looks at me. "I don't think it works that way. Here, let's meditate. It will slow our heart rates and help promote clarity of thought."

Henry looks at Zeb.

Zeb begins. *"Fabulae non morietur potest somnus solum legendas."*

It's the incantation from the chamber below the chapel. Guess it was the first thing Zeb could think of.

Henry looks at me and shrugs. I decide to chime in.

"Fabulae non morietur potest somnus solum legendas." Even though I am still chanting, I peek an eye out to Henry.

Then we both try not to laugh. We try to be serious.

Then it seems like the vibration coming out of our lungs, our bodies, our chant, turns inside out and starts actually vibrating the floor. Then harder. Then harder. Then the walls. Then the ceiling!

Shake. Shake shake.

Shake shake shake. Henry and I look at each other, terrified.

Is that an earthquake? I can't think of a worse place to be in an earthquake.

Shake. Shake.

Shaaaaake.

Henry and I panic. Zeb keeps chanting. Dust is flying off the ceiling now, hitting him on the head. Nope. Keeps chanting. Laser focus.

And then we see it.

"Well, kids! You tried! Sometimes that's all a lad can do! Or a lassie!" Henry and I jump in our seats. Zeb keeps chanting. I don't even think he felt the earthquake.

There, in the corner of the basecave, stands Beaumont, corncob pipe in hand.

"Darn tootin'." He nods. "Fancy chant. What are you, a bunch of witches? Wizards? Warlocks?! How'd you like that earthquake? That was my idea. I always did like a good shaker! Gits the blood pumping!"

"Yes, yes. Here, here." August and Sturdy agree with him, tipping their respective hats.

Plum leans in, kind. "Now, children, please forgive Beaumont and his rather tiresome antics—"

"Tiresome! Why, dear wife of mine, I been dead over a hundred years and I still ain't tired!" Beaumont exclaims.

"Aren't we all tired? Tired of this endless circus of banality. This indifferent march? This petty game of material stakes, all of which will someday, inevitably, be rendered meaningless . . .

each of us a grain of sand on an endless sea, a raindrop in a light-ning storm, a snowflake in a blinding blizzard—"

"A chicken with a gizzard!"

"What?"

"I can make up poems, too!" Beaumont goes on, slapping his knee. "A chicken with a gizzard! A wart on a lizard!"

"I was in the middle of—"

"Saying something depressing! Yeah, we git it! The world is terrible and we should all just throw ourselves off the nearest bridge. But don't listen to that hogwash, young'uns! This world is a blinding beauty; we live on a beautiful blue marble in the sky, revolving around a star. Ain't that just bonkers?!"

Henry continues trying to squiggle his mouth out from the tape.

Plum chimes in. "Children, what Beaumont here is trying to tell you is—"

"Live it up a little! Dagnabbit! This world is for the livers! And not the chicken livers like my two boys here!" Beaumont gestures to August and Sturdy.

"Oh, I do love a good foie gras," August reminisces.

"Exquisite, exquisite. With a bit of port," Sturdy agrees.

"Jeez-em-peets! You're hopeless!" Beaumont shakes his head.

Now Maxine floats above us. We look up, except Zeb who continues, now deep in trance. "*Fabulae non morietur potest som-nus solum legendas.*"

"Children, your freeeeedom hinges on your intellect . . ." And as Maxine says it, she simply flies up, fading into the dusty ceiling.

"Don't forget it, kids!" Now Beaumont starts singing to himself. "A chicken with a gizzard. A duck on a lizard. A frog in a blizzard."

Now the silly song fades and all the ghosts follow Maxine up, fading into whatever is up there, which I realize might involve a lot of spiders.

Don't think about the spiders. Don't think about the spiders.

Henry finally manages to wriggle his tape off the side of his mouth.

"Well. That was unneccesarily complicated," he comments.

"Henry, we have to get out of here! No vents. Aka, no oxygen." I nod toward the walls.

"It appears you are correct, dear sister," Henry agrees.

"We should all just hop our chairs over and gnaw the ropes with our teeth like rats," Zeb offers.

Henry and I contemplate this.

"Um, really?" I ask.

"Do you have a better idea?" Zeb asks.

"Actually," Henry chimes in, "if we can rub our ropes together the friction should wear them away. We just need to get closer to one another."

"Sounds better than a mouthful of rope," Zeb concedes.

"Okay," I agree.

The three of us begin hopping madly toward one another, our chairs jolting up and down like Mexican jumping beans. Hop. Scratch. Hop. Scratch. Hop.

Zeb's chair begins to tip over. I watch as, in a kind of slow motion, it teeters over and then:

THUMP.

"Ouch. Ouchity ouch ouch ouch. Okay, I'm okay," Zeb assures us.

But now Henry's chair crashes down beside him.

SLAM.

"Okay, that's gotta hurt," Zeb comments.

"Indeed," Henry agrees. But their chairs have come down precisely where they need to. Henry's and Zeb's wrists are right next to each other. Henry starts rubbing his wrist against Zeb's. "It would appear they've used garden-variety clothesline here. A lucky break. A heavier rope might take forever to—"

One layer of rope falls away from Zeb's wrists. "I seriously want to be you when I grow up, man," Zeb swoons. Only this time I'm not so grumbly about it.

"Our freedom hinges on our intellect," Henry says, pondering the advice from our ancestor ghosts. "I mean, quite frankly, that seems obvious."

"I know," I agree. "Kind of like 'the early bird gets the worm' or 'two wrongs don't make a right' or—"

"Never trust a man with a peg leg," Zeb adds.

"Okay, that is not an expression," I reply.

"It absolutely is," Zeb argues.

"In what world is that an expression?" I ask.

"I dunno. Mine, I guess?"

"I mean, like, did you grow up on a pirate ship on the open seas?" I kid.

"Yeah, and that was the expression. 'Never trust a man with a peg leg.' I can't believe you've never heard that."

"Yes, it's like that famous old expression, 'don't blow your nose too close to a chicken,'" I offer. "Or 'jump on a log, eat a hog.'"

"Everyone says that," Henry jokes. The last rope falls away "There. Got it!"

Henry's arms spring free and, in a flurry, he unties Zeb's wrists.

Now the two of them untie my wrists and we begin untying our ankles.

"Okay, how are we getting out of here? Any ideas? Anyone? Anyone? Anyone?" Zeb asks.

"There doesn't appear to be any ventilation." I look around. "Not one slat."

"That door looks pretty sturdy." Zeb nods toward the dark wood door with wrought-ron stylings.

"Wait a minute." I look at the door, formulating a thought.

Henry looks at me.

We say it simultaneously.

"Our freedom *hinges* on our intellect!!"

Zeb just looks at us.

"The hinges!" I explain. "The hinges of the door! I mean,

yes it has that scary wrought-iron lock but I bet if we—"

By the time I am through with my sentence, Henry is already at the hinges, investigating.

"Oh, I see. That makes sense." He peers into the inner workings of the hinges. "If we just loosen this part, we can take this pin out of here and . . ."

There is the smashing of one of the chairs and the fashioning of a makeshift tool. Blah blah, yadda yadda, Henry fumbles with the top hinge, taking out the wrought-iron pin with a flourish.

"Voilà!" The top hinge unfastens.

Zeb and I rush over, unfastening the pins on the two bottom hinges in a dash.

"If my calculations are correct, the door will now come off—"

"Lookout!" I scream.

The dark wood heavy door timbers over in giant . . .

THWAM!

The dust flies up around it and the sound echoes through the stone chamber.

"Uh-oh. We better get out of here before those tweedles come running." Zeb looks around.

"Indeed," Henry agrees.

"But which way?" I ask. The dark hallway stretches both ways into eternity.

"If memory serves, I believe I heard Binky heading to the left," Henry remembers.

"Are you serious right now?" I ask. "You're saying you could *hear* that."

"Dead serious," he adds.

From the end of the corridor echoes the sound of heavy footsteps. They must have heard the door crash. Everybody in California must have heard the door crash.

"Okay, no time for chitchat. Let's go!" Zeb snaps us into shape and the three of us take off, running in the opposite direction of the footsteps.

Behind us, the footsteps come closer.

As we make our way through the dark, dank labyrinth of the basement, we hear the noise echoing behind us.

"Come out, come out, little kids!"

"Come out wherever you are!"

Great. Hide-and-seek. I hate that game.

Mostly because I am very, very bad at it.

18

THE HALLWAY DEPOSITS us at the bottom of a rickety wooden staircase. Behind us, we can still hear the footsteps of the guards in pursuit. The three of us hurl ourselves up the steps, about thirty of them, and through a door, shutting it behind us and locking it. In front of us is a kind of mini courtyard. Vines and stone benches.

"Which way?" I ask.

Henry points to a doorway across the courtyard. That way.

The three of us fling ourselves through the doorway and into the room, catching our breath.

"Shh." We listen. "They're out there."

Outside we can hear the steps of two guards, looking around.

"Hey, this way!" The two guard's feet hit the ground and

the sound gets farther and farther away.

"Phew." Zeb exhales.

"I wonder why they didn't check in here?" I ask.

"They likely assumed we wanted to escape, and there were two passageways from the courtyard out," Henry quips.

"Ah, so you tricked them by doing the thing no one would do." Zeb thinks.

"Exactly." Henry nods.

Zeb and I share a look. "Not bad."

"I vant to be alone." The voice breaks into our little moment. It's a woman's voice, a kind of European accent to it.

We look over and observe, for the first time, the room we're in. It's a kind of dressing room, with tuxedos, assorted costumes, boas, hats, and evening gowns hanging from all four corners. In the middle of the wall on the other side of the room sits a solitary figure facing the other way. We can only see her reflection in the mirror. She shimmers a beautiful gray-blue.

"I vant to be alone," she repeats.

"Cool! Look at these costumes!" Zeb says, donning a top hat.

He doesn't see the ghost before us. The ghost of Greta Garbo, sitting there on the vanity in some kind of white chiffon getup, making her look like a shimmering dove.

"Greta Garbo?"

She looks up at us, and says in the same Swedish accent, "I vant to be alone."

Henry and I step forward, transfixed. Zeb, on the other

hand, is now playing with a boa.

She looks at us, imploring, "You must reverse the incantation. Your little spell . . . or I shall never have any peace."

Henry and I look at each other.

I guess it never occurred to us that our little incantation might actually *bother* some of the ghosts. Our ancestors seem to relish making an entrance, telling us strange things, and— poof!—disappearing once again. But I guess you never really know when it comes to ghosts. They're as finicky and singular as . . . well, people.

Henry nods to the Greta Garbo ghost. "Yes, yes, of course. We didn't know we were . . . actually bothering you. Or upsetting you—"

She begins to fade into the mirror, her reflection a prism of light and shadows. "I vant to be alone. . . ."

"Henry, do you think we hurt the ghosts by saying the incantation?" I ask.

"I don't know. But we can't forget to reverse it." Henry turns to Zeb. "Zeb, don't let us forget to reverse the incantation."

Zeb is now wearing a top hat and a boa and wielding a sword. He steps forward, declaring, "I shan't, my noble king!"

"Okay, you're having far too much fun right now, considering the circumstances."

He shrugs. "Just trying to be present for the universe."

"Okay, I don't mean to be a bummer, but we still have a heist to thwart, remember?"

"I know, I know. I'm waiting for you guys to finish your

ghost encounter." He thrusts his sword in the air. "And then I shall march with honor!"

"Fine. Let's march with honor this way." Henry leads us out to the courtyard, following the cobblestone path.

We take a left and full stop, stepping all over one another as we see three guards up the path about a baseball field away. We twirl on a dime and head the opposite direction of the guards.

"Phew. That was close," Zeb whispers.

The three of us breathe a sigh of relief but we should just take that breath back because just as we take a quick left, we run smack-dab into the Midwestern Mastermind.

19

"AH! JUST THE three little annoying nuisances I was looking for!" The Midwestern Mastermind towers over us.

Up close, now, I see he really is one of the skinniest people I have ever encountered. The purple rings around his eyes are more defined, and his snaggly yellow teeth look like a row off a corncob.

In case we had any thought of escape, behind him are the majority of the tweedle-guards. Most of them are lugging things around and groaning, but a few of them, about three, are most definitely on surly guard duty. Sitting a few feet away, looking bored and playing *Candy Crush*, is Binky.

"Binky? I thought you hated video games!" Zeb looks over.

"Yeah, that was an act for your bleeding-heart dad." She rolls her eyes.

He stares at her for a beat, the air between them heavy. "I can't believe you! You are literally the worst! I can't believe I was looking forward to spending Christmas with you! Now I wouldn't even accept anything from you! Not an Xbox One X! Or even a kids' motorcycle. Or one of those things that you drive around and has bars on the top—"

"Dune buggy," I chime in.

"A dune buggy! Or even a golf cart! Or an all-inclusive safari on the Serengeti! Or a robot butler named Jeeves! Or a—"

"Are you done?" the Midwestern Mastermind interrupts.

"Not quite. No, not quite at all. I left out the most important thing, the number one thing, I would not accept from you. Your love! I would not accept your love!" Zeb shouts.

"Got it. So—"

"NO LOVE!" Zeb cuts off the Mastermind.

Some of the other tweedle-guards are coming over now, taking an interest.

"What's the deal?" one of them asks the one nearest.

"I think that lady was the bride in this sham of a wedding and I think she was gonna be his stepmom," the other guard answers.

"Man. Stepmoms suck," a tweedle answers.

"I hear ya," the other agrees.

"Would you idiots mind!" Mastermind insults them. "Can't you see; I'm wrapping up a heist here?!"

He turns to us, smiling. "That's right, kids. Wrapping up. That means . . . success. That means . . . on your part . . . failure."

"Failure is just a stepping stone to success," Zeb corrects him.

"No! No, it's not! This. Is. A. Fail. You lost! Okay, get it through your heads! Losers!" Mastermind now calms down, taking another tone.

He steps forward, closer to us. "You know, I was thinking about you kids. What's the best thing to do with little obnoxious kids that won't go away?"

"Well, I wouldn't say we're obnoxious. Especially Henry, he's very polite," Zeb points out.

"Stop it! Stop interrupting me!" He goes back to his calm act. "And I realized . . . Yes, you can kill those kids. You can. String 'em up by their little belt loops. But . . . is that really the most profitable thing to do . . . ? I mean, wouldn't it be better just to keep these little kids as your very own personal servants? Living a full life in the basement, eating gruel and doing whatever I say for eternity? Isn't that a more suitable punishment?"

Henry and I look at each other.

Mastermind goes on. "After all, they're certainly smarter than these idiots I've hired."

"Hey!" One of the guards takes offense.

"I'm just telling it like it is. I could use some indentured servants with brains." He scruffs Henry's hair. Henry winces. "And . . . now that I'm going to have the most enormous mansion and estate in the history of the world, I could use a sweet little girl to clean it! Just like little girls are supposed to do, ain't that right?" Now he scruffs my hair. I fume.

"And you, little blue-streaked devil. I'm sure I'll be able to turn you into a juvenile delinquent in no time." He goes to scruff Zeb's hair.

"Don't touch me, dude," Zeb tells him.

He sneers, drawing back. "Oh, don't worry, little ones. You'll make a great little troupe. Perhaps I can teach you to do funny acts for my many guests. A kind of 'in-house' theater."

"I wouldn't have pegged him for a theater guy," I whisper.

He turns to his tweedle-guards.

"All right, knuckleheads, load 'em in the truck." Two tweedle-guards come forward, grabbing Henry and Zeb.

None of the tweedles seem to want to grab me so Binky, annoyed, does it for them, pulling me by the arm.

The back of the very last white truck is open, revealing a treasure trove of statues and oil paintings. The guards begin leading Henry and Zeb over to the mouth of the truck, which waits to swallow us whole.

It never occurred to me that we might fail. That somehow, after all this effort, all this madcap running around, running back and forth, communing with ghosts, trying to save every-one . . . that it would all be for naught. That's not the way it is in movies. In movies, no matter what, the good guys win.

Like, in that movie with all the airplanes flying around in Dunkirk, when all the normal people give up their boats to go save the trapped soldiers because Churchill—

Wait a minute.

Churchill.

Winston Churchill showed up in the bathtub and he said what? What?

The guards hoist Zeb up into the truck. Henry looks back at me.

Strategy!

Strategy strategy strategy . . .

Before my head knows what my body is doing, I hoist off Binky's arm, tipping her off-balance.

"Hey!" she screeches.

I rush over to the cab of the truck, using the side mirror as a ladder, stepping up onto the top of the cab, and then onto the top of the truck.

"You imbeciles! Get her!" the Mastermind shouts.

The tweedle-guards circle in, now there are about twenty of them, almost the whole crew.

"Okay, okay, I'll come down. I'll come down in a second and there doesn't have to be a struggle. Okay? I'll come down." The tweedles relax a bit.

Henry and Zeb look up at me like I've lost my marbles.

"But before I do . . . I just want to say one thing." I take a breath. "Look behind me! What do you see? A castle? Or a testament to one man's greed? I mean, seriously, did he really need ALL THAT STUFF?"

The tweedles look up at me quizzically.

"And this guy, your boss! Look at him! Does *he* really need all that stuff? Does anyone? No. I say no! And I say . . . that if you guys are the ones doing all the work, all the toil, all the blood, sweat, and tears . . . then this guy, your boss, shouldn't be the one making off with all the profits. You get me? The great Charlie Chaplin organized his artists, he stood up to the man, and said, 'No more! *We* are the power! Not you!'"

The tweedles shuffle a bit on their feet.

"I say you should do the same!" I shout.

"C'mon! Get her down!" the Mastermind urges.

"Look, some of you are getting paid as little as two thousand, right?"

The tweedles shuffle some more.

"Get! Her! Down!" The diabolical Midwesterner is now steaming at the ears.

"I don't know much but I do know that *he*!" I point at the hopping-mad mastermind. "*He* . . . is raking in millions from this. Maybe even billions!"

The tweedles start looking at one another, sharing glances.

"So, does that seem fair to you? This guy? Here? This skinny little guy? The guy who has been verbally abusing you for the past three hours? He's just sailing out of this set for life . . . and what about you? What about your rent? Your car payments? Your medical bills? Your dumb roommate situations? Are you set for life? Are you waltzing out of here? Well . . . are you?"

The tweedles mutter a response.

"Are you?"

"No!" One of the tweedle-guards yells it out.

Now another. "No way!"

"Not even close!"

"I just saved a bunch of money switching my car insurance!"

Everybody looks at that guy.

"Sorry."

But the tweedle crowd is riled up now, seeing the injustice of it all. I roll with it.

"And is *he*!" I point back to the Midwestern Mastermind. "Is *he* going to serve all your sentences for you if you get caught? Well . . . is he?"

"No!"

"Nope!"

"Are you kidding?"

"No way!"

They're one-upping one another. Rapid. Ready to pounce. All the injustices of the world suddenly revealed.

I go on. "And if we stick together, we can help one another. We can demand fair payment, and stick it to the man! Say it with me! Enough is enough! Enough is enough!"

"Enough is enough!" they shout out.

"Enough is enough!" Now everyone.

It's kind of fun.

The Midwestern Mastermind starts to tiptoe backward, trying to melt into the bushes.

"Oh, no you don't!" One of the tweedle-guards grabs him, pinning him down. "You're staying right there, you greedy little jerk!"

"Yeah, you jerk!"

"How about share the wealth!"

"Yeah, how about giving a working guy a break, huh?"

I pipe up. "Now, you guys, it's not too late. You could just set yourselves free and just take off! There are even costumes on the first floor, next to the courtyard! You could dress up as wedding guests and just flee to liberty, away from this dark life of thievery and woe . . . ! Also, you should free the wedding guests!"

"Oh, they're not going anywhere," one of the tweedles says.

"Why not?" Henry asks.

"They're watching a *Law & Order* marathon," he answers. "We put it on at the beginning of the heist. You know, just to put everybody at ease. . . . That show's really good. Good acting. Gripping plot. Sam Waterston offers a certain gravitas. . . ."

Another tweedle joins in. "That noise at the beginning. *Clunk. Clunk.* It's like you have to watch."

"Oh yeah. Exactly. They get you in the first two minutes," another tweedle agrees.

"Wait a minute." It comes to me. "So those gunshots we heard were from a *Law & Order* marathon?"

"Gunshots? Yeah, that definitely wasn't us." The tweedle thinks. "Must have been the episode with the fancy art thief and his mistress."

Now another tweedle pipes up. "No, it was definitely the one with prep school kids and the measles mom."

"Oh, that was a good one."

"I know, right?" The tweedles nod in agreement.

Down below, both Binky and the Midwestern Mastermind are being tied to a tree. Both of them are kicking and hurling insults.

"You imbecile!" Binky yells. "You ruined my entire impeccable plan! You blew it!! I should have left you in Kalamazoo!"

"Not everyone has your snake-in-the-grass talents, Ms. Royal Princess Bride! No, they do not. But I was the one down here in the gutter recruiting muscle while you . . . you were having *cake tastings!*"

Binky gasps. "I did that for us! You know my sensitivity to carbs!"

But bicker as they might, they're literally stuck together for the foreseeable future.

"Sorry, dude, shoulda been less greedy," one of the tweedles tells him as he tightens the rope. The others chant:

"Enough is enough! Enough is enough!"

This scene of egalitarian happiness is interrupted, however, by the sound of sirens in the distance.

Finally.

The cops.

"Oh, dudes, we better get out of here!" The tweedles all realize this is not the best place to be right now. It's amazing how quickly they scatter to all four corners of the map, into the trees, into the castle, up the hills, down to the sea. It's about twenty seconds until every last one of them is gone completely, leaving our resistance moment all but a giddy memory.

The line of police cars winds its way up the long drive to the castle, snaking its way up to us in flashes of blue and red.

The rain has gone back down to a drizzle, almost a mist.

"Wait a minute." Zeb stands up.

Henry and I look, seeing what he sees. In the first police car, in the front seat, there sits the Redondo guard. Right there, in the passenger seat. He smiles wide.

As the car pulls up, the Redondo guard gets out, hurrying over to Zeb.

"Hey, little dude!" He gives him a fist bump.

Zeb fist-bumps back. "What are you even doing here? I'm so confused!"

"Oh, little dude." Redondo goes on. "I realized something up there on that ledge. I'm not a bad guy. I'm a good guy who just never got a chance to show it. But you saw that in me. You gave me the opportunity to learn who I am. And for that, I'm giving you this certificate for two large two-topping cheese pizzas."

He hands Zeb a coupon.

"Okay, I know it's not much but, well, heck, I don't have much."

"No." Zeb looks down at the coupons. "I love pizza. Are you kidding?"

"Also, I remember that skinny dude, the boss guy, he told us 'leave no witnesses.' Like, in a really mean voice, 'leave no witnesses.' It was like diabolical." Redondo guy shakes his head.

"I couldn't let them do that. Not to my little dude!" He scruffs Zeb's hair. Zeb smiles.

The police cars start making their way up the path, parking in a circle, blocking off the area. Two of the policemen come walking up. The Redondo guard nods to Binky and the Midwestern Mastermind tied to a tree.

"That's them." He points to them.

The cops walk over. "You have the right to remain silent. Anything you say can and will be used—"

"So, what are you going to do now?" Zeb looks up at Redondo.

"You know, don't make fun of me, but I think I'm going to become a cop," Redondo answers.

"Seriously?"

"Sure, dude. If I have to look at one more dirty dish left by my roommate, I'll lose it. Besides. I kind of like being a good guy."

He looks around at the blue-and-red circle flashing around all of us.

The cops escort the Midwestern Mastermind and Binky off into their respective cars.

Zeb jumps up, running over to the Midwestern Mastermind, sitting in the squad car.

Zeb leans in and does his impeccable impression of the Midwestern Mastermind: "Hi, ya, so, I just got busted pulling off the dumbest heist in history. I'm basically an idiot!"

The Midwestern Mastermind looks up at him, realizing Zeb was imitating him the whole night, screwing up all his master plans.

"You! It was you! You're the one giving all those stupid commands to my stupid army of dimwits!"

Zeb nods, relishing it. "See. Just like I said. Failure is a stepping stone to success."

The Midwestern Mastermind fumes.

The car begins to drive off.

Zeb yells after it: "Stepping stone to success!"

20

THE THREE OF us wait at the top of the driveway for Zeb's dad and his crew of waylaid heroes to return. The police have informed us that the roads have been closed but that they shouldn't have taken matters into their own hands in the first place.

"See. That's what I said!" I exclaim.

"Yes, well." The policeman states, "This was a police matter. No need for citizens to get involved."

"Wait. Was there even a violent uprising down the hill?" Henry asks.

"No. There was no violent uprising. Clearly, this was just a ploy to get your father and the rest of the able-bodied folks down the hill. A ploy that worked perfectly." The officer's voice is official.

"So, everybody was just totally fooled?" Zeb asks.

"Precisely," the cop replies.

"Well, what about the treasure? Is it all gone?" I wonder.

"Not exactly. They only got as far as Ventura. Where they got stuck in traffic. I guess this villain, despite all his preparations—"

"*Her* preparations," I correct.

"—neglected to take into account the soul-crushing traffic jams of the Los Angeles metropolitan area." The policeman is really seeming to enjoy this. "It was a rookie mistake."

"But where were they going?" I ponder.

"Probably the Port of Los Angeles. It is the busiest port in America. He could have shoved the treasures into a shipping container, and off they go over the high seas. Sell them to shady investors in a foreign land." He squints. "But thanks to you kids, nothing went as planned."

We three look at one another.

"Well, thanks, Officer." We smile.

"I'm sure there's some medals in this for you somewhere. You saved the Hearst estate millions of dollars." He looks out at a line of cars coming up the road. "Well, kiddos, looks like your folks are back."

We follow his gaze and there before us return all the heroes and heroines fooled into going down the mountain to save the day.

"Dad!" Zeb runs down the hill, embracing his father.

"Zeb! Oh thank God! Thank God you're okay!" He looks around. "Where's Binky?"

Henry and I look at each other, each of us making our own respective squiggle mouth.

"Awk-ward," I whisper.

"No joke," Henry whispers back. "Maybe we should step backward in a casual fashion."

The two of us tiptoe backward, leaving Zeb to his difficult explanation.

By the time the police get up to the wedding hall to "liberate" the guests, they are on their ninth episode of *Law & Order*. Even when the head policeman goes to make an announcement, they shush him, not wanting him to interrupt the cliffhanger.

Henry and I look at each other.

"Wow. That must be some show," I say.

Henry shrugs. "TV, shmeevee."

"At least it kept them company while they were held captive," I suggest.

"Did it? Or was it just another example of the infinite distraction Aldous Huxley warned us about? A distraction so great, mind you, that it quelled the uprising of actual hostages? And, one might argue, aren't all these things, whether a TV show, a film, a video game, an app . . . don't they all add up to the infinite distraction that is quelling us all, as the one percent, whether they be CEOs, multinational corporations, or

Midwestern Masterminds, rob each and every one of us, transferring all the wealth from the distracted masses to their own greedy little coffers?" Henry points out.

"Wow." I contemplate this. Then I notice the copious amounts of food and beverages still left over from the reception. "We should probably . . . have a party?"

Henry looks at me.

"What?" I defend myself. "We thwarted a heist, Henry. We have a castle, food, drinks, people, a DJ . . . and something to celebrate."

"What DJ?" he asks.

"That guy!" I point to the spiky-haired DJ guy packing up his records. "Hey, you!"

I run over, begging him to stay. He shrugs. "Sure. Whatever."

He places his boxes of records back down and puts his headphones on, cueing something up. Then he grabs the microphone, winks at us, and addresses the room.

"Ladies and gentlemen, I would just like to announce that you are officially liberated from . . . whatever all *that* was. And you have the right to remain . . . awesome!" He puts the needle on the record.

The cavernous space explodes with the sound of thumping bass. Suddenly, the wedding guests, now joined by the returned thwarted heroes, swarm the dance floor, happy to finally be having some fun after a long night. The dance floor explodes, balloons are dropped, and champagne bottles are popped.

Henry looks at me.

"Eva, there is one last thing we have to do."

21

THE EGYPTIAN NEW Kingdom statue stands looking out into the night. I guess this one was too heavy for the Mastermind and his tweedle army.

Henry and I approach it and it starts to tremble. Suddenly, the ground around us is covered in smoke, so it's impossible to see, and we hear the sound of a voice, singular, from within.

"Why you little scamps! You surely fooled 'em!"

Beaumont appears through the smoke.

"Dear children, once again, you have persevered." Plum waves her fan, fanning the smoke toward Beaumont, who coughs.

"Goshdarnit, Plum! You're choking me to death!"

"How can she choke you to death when you're already

dead?" Maxine purrs from next to the onyx statue.

"Well put, well put." August and Sturdy clink martini glasses.

"Y'all are in cahoots! Everyone's against me!" Beaumont jokes.

Henry steps forward. "We have to reverse the incantation. The ghosts can't rest in peace until we do."

"Well, what the heck did you think we're here for! Sightseeing?!" Beaumont asks.

"Well, how do we do it?" I ask.

"Oh, fair children, worry not. The key to all of this is simple. The dead shall rest in peace again," Plum assures us.

"Quite right, quite right," August and Sturdy agree.

Maxine leans in. "We are only death and shadows."

"Oh, here we go!" Beaumont interrupts.

"Weeeeee aaaaare oooooonly deeeeeeath and shaaaaadows." Maxine starts to fade into the smoke.

The other ghosts begin to fade, as well.

"*Pulvis et umbra sumus.*" Maxine's voice stays over the smoke. "*Puuuuuulvis et uuuuuumbra suuuuumus.*"

And now both the voice and the spirits are gone, faded into the night.

"That's it. That's how we reverse the incantation." Henry looks at me. "Got it? *Pulvis et umbra sumus.*"

I nod.

The two of us look at each other, nod, and turn toward Hearst Castle.

We say it together:

"*Pulvis et umbra sumus.*"

Then the two of us stand there, as if waiting for a sign.

But there is no sign.

Nothing.

Except, all the way up at the top of the outdoor landing, Zeb's head peeks out. "Guys, you have to see this. There's this really old grandma and she's breakdancing and it is *so* awesome!"

Henry and I look at each other and shrug.

Upstairs, the beat changes. There's the screech of synthesizers.

"Infinite distraction, here we come."

22

HONESTLY, I WOULD have liked to keep the ghosts around just a bit longer. To say thank you. To find Winston. And Humphrey. And Groucho. And Greta. To thank them. Also, honestly, to ask them a thousand questions about what it used to be like, how it used to be in this place.

And to see, maybe, if it could even be possible, to somehow see our parents again. Although I know that's a long shot.

Zeb is now up in the DJ booth, spinning records with the DJ, wearing a roman gladiator helmet.

"Do you think he stole that?" Henry ponders.

"Well, I think he'll put it back." I shrug. "It's probably the most fun that helmet has had in a long time."

Henry contemplates the dancing crowd.

"They really seem to be having the time of their lives."

"Henry, I'm sad we reversed the spell when we did," I admit.

"We had to. Don't you remember how sad Greta Garbo looked? 'I vant to be alone.'"

"I know but what if we could've—"

I cut myself off.

Henry looks at me.

"Our parents?"

I nod.

"Eva, remember what our mom said. 'We are with you always.'" He looks into my eyes. "And that love is the only thing . . . that is infinite."

I look back at him. We share a moment of acknowledgment. Yes, we are in this together.

"Eva, we are in this together."

It's like he read my mind. How did he do that? I look at him, feeling so stupid for being jealous. Territorial. Petty.

"Always and forever."

"I'm sorry I sort of freaked out. I don't understand feelings."

"Me neither." Henry smiles.

He hugs me and I hug him back, thankful that the world invented brothers.

This fine moment is interrupted by . . . an acrobatic stunt. From across the dance floor we see it: Zeb zip-lining from the giant wrought-iron chandelier directly into the wedding cake.

"The journey is the destinatiooooooooon!"

Splurtch.

Zeb rolls around, disoriented, in the demolished wedding cake. His gold Roman gladiator helmet sits slanted sideways on his head.

Henry and I look at each other.

"Wedding cake. Eight hundred dollars. Seeing Zeb covered in frosting. Priceless," I add.

Zeb waves up to the two of us, his eyes peering out through the white frosting like a sugar ghost. He licks the frosting off his own cheek.

"Hmm. Strawberry shortcake. I think those are real strawberries. *Guys, the strawberries are real!!*"

And I know, in this moment, with Zeb yelling about the real strawberries, with that octogenarian woman popping and locking in the middle of the dance floor, with Zeb's dad twirl-dancing the little flower girl, with the policeman trying out his not-so-great country line-dance moves, with Henry dutifully inspecting the strength of the banister, that the world is a good place, full of good people, and that there is more kindness and love in this world than all the gold in Hearst Castle.

ACKNOWLEDGMENTS

Thank you to my amazing editor, Kristen Pettit, who has elevated my work on so many occasions. Thank you to Rosemary Stimola, my amazing agent, for believing in this series. Of course, my mom, dad, sister, and brother . . . you are my nearest and dearest. And an enormous thank-you to my incredible husband, Sandy Tolan, who has been supportive of me in every way. A final thanks to my little boy, Wyatt, who is the reason I wrote these very books.